I0760588

Of The Deep

Mermaid Anthology

K.M. Robinson
Elle Beaumont
Amber R. Duell
E.J. Hagadorn

Published by Crescent Sea Publishing.
www.crescentseapublishing.com

Cover designed by Reading Transforms.

persons, living or dead, is entirely coincidental and beyond the intent of either the author or the publisher.

Dedication

To all of you mermaid dreamers,
never give up—
you're mermazing!

The *Of the Deep* mermaid Anthology has been close to our hearts since the moment we decided to create a collection of works from the depths of the seas. Our authors, both established and emerging, have created incredible tails from under the, and we hope you enjoy diving into them as much as we did.

Within this printed edition, you'll also find the artwork of serveral highly talented individuals who gave their time and effort to bring this book to life through their artwork. We couldn't be more thrilled!

We hope you enjoy your time with us beneath the waves.

Let's dive in!

MY SKIN TINGLES UNDER THE DEEP RAYS OF THE SUN AS I stretch out on the castle steps. The edges of the water cascade over my fins—a stark contrast to the warm rays of light.

I shiver in delight.

Jarek runs his fingers over my hair, tangling them in my locks as he brushes my tresses. His boots rest near my head and I lazily rest my arm over his feet. I smile up at him, returning his grin before he looks out at the sea.

"That sounds magical, Aila," Jarek remarks in a far-off voice. "I wish I could see that."

"Perhaps one day you will, Jarek," Persephone leans over, resting her head on the prince's shoulder.

"I've known you for four years, Seph, and never once have I been able to swim far enough or hold my breath long enough to visit your realm," he replies sadly. "It's just my luck that I would end up with two such optimistic best friends. I'll never be able to visit you though—at least, not beneath the surface."

"Which is why we come to *you,* our friend," I say, pushing myself upright. I rest a hand on his knee, gently lowering my chin.

"You know I adore your visits," he recovers, offering a smile. His eyes are still sad.

Jarek looks transfixed on something out in the water. When I turn, a ship sails in the distance, so far away that it's a foggy mass embedded in the clouds of the setting sun.

"You girls should probably go home," Jarek sighs. "It will be dark soon and you don't want to get caught during feeding time."

Traveling in the dark doesn't scare mer, but traveling when the sharks make their way in to find their dinner is a terrifying experience.

"We'll be fine, Jarek," Seph tries to convince him. "Just a few more minutes."

"No," he shakes his head. "I must insist that you go. You can come visit me again soon."

He stands to his feet, nearly knocking Persephone and I off balance. The prince retreats up the steps to the landing at the top of the concrete staircase leading to the water. He produces something shiny, holding it up for us before he walks back down the stairs.

"Take this to your grandfather, Aila, as a sign of our

respect."

He places a golden ring in my hand encrusted in pearls. The sunlight glints off it, flaring into my eyes. I run my fingers over the intricate design.

"If you put it on your thumb, it will make it harder to lose," he smirks. "You both have such tiny hands."

"Delicate," Persephone corrects him, making him chuckle.

"Off you go," he nods toward the ocean. "I'll see you ladies again soon."

We wave before slipping off of the steps and dropping into the water. The water surrounding my face, pulling my hair away from my body as I descend into the ocean, is comforting and refreshing.

"I don't like that we can't stay longer," Persephone complains as she locates the midwater squids we brought with us to guide us home in the limited light. Once we reach the dark depths, they will glow a pale moonlight green, illuminating our path as we swim. Of course, we can see without them, but they're comforting to have with us.

"We have to go home sometime, cousin," I remind her. I was always the responsible one among us. "Besides, now we have a mission."

I flick my hand at her, showing off the ring.

"I'm not sure why he gave it to *you,*" she grumbles.

"I'm more responsible," I inform her playfully.

"Palace Steps"
by Millenium Genesis

"It's probably because you have bigger hands," she shoots back, darting ahead as we swim.

The ring suddenly feels heavier on my finger as I swim to catch up to her, her blue tail glittering in the light from the setting sun. Eventually, she gives up resisting and speaks to me again, chattering the rest of the way home.

Upon arriving, I dart into the palace grotto. The roascea colony floating at the top of the grotto resembles the chandelier from Jarek's palace window. Their long, glowing tentacles sway with the movement of the water.

"Grandfather?" I call, knowing he's somewhere in the palace walls. "Grandfather?"

I find him tucked away in his study, pouring over the rock garden he had built in the shape of the kingdom. He smiles, motioning me inside when he notices me floating in the open entryway.

"Aila," he says softly. "How was your trip to the surface?"

"It was nice, grandfather. Jarek sent something for you."

I wriggle the gold ring off my finger.

"And how is Prince Jarek doing? Is he well?"

"He is," I reply, handing over the gift. "This is a sign of his respect."

My grandfather examines the ring, finally placing it on his right hand.

"Jarek has always been a good boy. He'll make a fine man someday and an even better king."

Persephone would give Grandfather an earful if she heard him call the prince a boy. He's eighteen, as are we, though I understand Grandfather's point more than my cousin would—we're still young, even for our years.

A small school of fish buzzes into the room, darting in and immediately back out when they notice us. The tiniest wave reaches out to me after a moment from the water they displaced by their sudden movements. It feathers over my skin just enough to notice it.

"This was a lovely gesture—I'm impressed he remembered the celebration. Please thank him for me," my grandfather adds. "Actually, perhaps you could take this back to him to give his mother."

He hands a conch shell message. It will whisper the queen's name, directing anyone who finds it to give it to the proper recipient. When she listens to it, it will repeat my grandfather's words only once before fizzling off like foam washing out of the ocean onto the sand.

"I can take it tomorrow," I promise, taking the conch from him. I clutch it to my chest.

"Very good. You should get some rest. It would be wise to deliver it in the morning since we're so busy tomorrow afternoon. It's a little early, but you could use the extra sleep anyway," he sends me off.

Inside my room, I place the note in my jewelry box. The shells encrusting the rectangle are familiar under my palms as I open the lid. The note rests against my hair jewels, waiting for me to wake.

I untangle the hair comb from my locks, having become entwined in my tresses when Jarek ran his finger absentmindedly over them like he might pet one of the dogs I've seen running the palace grounds. A few strands of my hair rip out when I pull it away, but I can remove them from the turquoise comb tomorrow.

I love traveling with my cousin, but it would be nice to have some alone time tomorrow while I swim to the surface. I'll leave before Persephone can wake up.

I float over to my bed and pull the seaweed blanket over my tail, nestling in for the night.

By the time I surface, the sun is over the horizon, dousing the entire world in brilliant shades of pink and orange. The sunlight reflects off of the palace walls, dancing back at me as it twinkles.

The opalescent shine to the outside of the palace amazes

me every time I see it—it's more radiant than anything we have under the sea. To be fair, they don't have the coral reefs we have, so I suppose it's almost an even trade.

As I swim closer to the stairs connecting land and sea, I notice Jarek's head bobbing in the water. He treads in a circle, searching for something.

Suddenly, another person rises out of the water, wrapping their arms around his neck. The girl pulls him close. He chuckles, wrapping his arms around her.

I pause, feeling uncomfortable approaching him while he's with someone.

Why didn't he tell me?

They bob in the water together, slowly spinning in the sunrise. His back is to me when I finally recognize her —Persephone.

She tangles her hands in his hair, drawing him closer. My cousin whispers something to him as they spin slowly, bobbing with the waves.

I splash back in the water when she kisses him, pulling his mouth to hers. Praying the sound of my movements mixed with the splash of the waves against my back, I wait.

Unfortunately, they turn, spotting me against the blue water. Jarek pales when he sees me, but Persephone only freezes for a moment before tipping the prince's head toward her and kissing his lips one more time.

She swims to me, leaving him behind in the waves as if nothing is wrong. Her smile makes me uncomfortable.

"Hi, Aila." She ducks her head under the water, wetting her hair to make it easier to slick back.

"I…" I mumble, blinking back my confusion.

"Why are you here?" she asks sweetly, trying to distract me.

"Grandfather sent a message to the queen," I hold up the conch.

She snatches it from my hand and swims quickly over to Jarek who is still watching us. My cousin hands it to him before darting back to me. She grabs my wrist and drags me under the water.

I look over my shoulder—having no control over my other movements—and see Jarek's feet as he kicks his way back to the shore.

"Persephone, what was that?" I ask when she finally slows as we reach the bed of seaweed near the ocean floor. It waves to us, beckoning us to play.

"Nothing," she claims. "What was grandfather's shell about?"

I truthfully had no idea what he wanted, but that wasn't the point.

"You were kissing Jarek," I try to keep the confusion out of my voice but to no avail.

"Yes," she looks back at me, finally releasing my wrist.

"But Jarek has never been interested in us. After all,

mer and humans can never be together," I try to process the situation.

"We can," she announces stubbornly. A lock of her hair floats in front of her face prompting her to angrily brush it back in the water.

"You can...*what*?"

"We can be together—Jarek and I. I'm going to make it happen."

"How?" I stop swimming, putting my hands on my hips. I wish I had added a belt like grandfather's this morning to make me look more powerful and imposing, but at least my *iluse* was striking and fierce with its collection of netting, shells, and pearls on my chest. "You can't grow legs, you know, and he can't breathe underwater."

"We'll see about that," she mutters.

"Seph, you're being ridiculous. It can't happen." I use her family nickname to soften my words.

"We're in love, Aila," she shrieks. For a moment, it looks like she might want to take the words back, but with a slight shake of her head, she banishes those thoughts. She lowers her voice, seething. "We are in love, and we will be together—we'll make it so. You don't have to help me, but you *will* stay out of my way."

She turns, swimming off quickly. I think about going after her, but that would just lead to another fight. I take my time swimming back, not wanting to catch her, but still making sure to be back in time for the festival activities.

The Pearl Ball is held once a year after a week of celebrating. The festivities draw in the entire kingdom, and is not only a large source of income for the merpeople but also offers a well-deserved break.

The first day of the festivities starts slow, opening in the afternoon. For an entire week, mer flood into the palace district, resting their fins with any friend they can find for the duration of the celebration, often times staying at a different home every night.

"Wow, I…*just, wow*," Troy exclaims as he swims up to me, eyes wide.

I run my hands over my *iluse,* smoothing down the strands of pearls. This had been an outfit I had been saving for months for this occasion.

I try to smile as if nothing is wrong, but I fail miserably. Troy scoops me into his arms, twirling me around.

"You can't look like that and be unhappy," he says playfully. When I don't speak, he adds, "Okay, what is it? Tell me so I can fix it and we can go to the opening festivities."

I pause, debating whether to tell him. Troy and I

haven't been dating for very long, and while I trust him, it's still family business.

"I saw Persephone doing something I don't think she should be doing," I admit.

"Making out with Galon?" Troy teases, pulling me closer.

"No."

"Good. I hate that guy." Troy quirks his eyebrow flirtatiously at me. I personally wasn't a fan of Galon and his smugness either.

"She was kissing Jarek," I admit.

"The...prince?" He points up. The water his movement displaces, waves against his dark brown locks, making them sway magnificently. I nod at his reference. "How exactly does she plan on handling that one?"

"You see the problem," I sigh dramatically. "I think I need to tell grandfather—she's convinced they can be together and I just don't see how that could ever work."

"Your grandfather will know what to do," Troy assures me. "We can find him now before the events start."

He tugs at my hand, pulling me toward the festival about to begin in the waterways. His hand is warm and reassuring in mine. Aside from Jarek, Troy is my best guy friend and the perfect fit for me.

Halfway to the open ceremony location, I spot Persephone branching off from the crowd. She waves to a group of her friends, blowing kisses before she swishes her tail, leaving them in a trail of bubbles.

"Did you see—" Troy's words are cut off by my nod. "So we…"

"Are following her. Yes," I reply, changing course.

The sea dances turquoise—my favorite color—as we quietly follow behind my cousin. Beams of light filter from the surface the higher we get.

Instead of going to the palace, Persephone veers off to the right, taking a route I'm unfamiliar with.

"Do you know where we're going, darling?" Troy asks, pulling me close enough to wrap his arm around my waist. When his wrist hits a strand of pearls, he drops his hand lower.

A cold current chills me to my bones as we swim through it. Troy tries to lend me his warmth, but nothing helps the feel a mer gets from a current.

"I haven't been here before."

Everything around us gets dark. We push forward, following the remnants of the bubbles my cousin leaves in her wake. When we surface, we find ourselves inside a cavern.

The walls glow blue, little streaks of light crawling up the rocks. The water takes on a mystical hue, glowing with the reflection of the spores on the wall.

Persephone's arms rest on the edge of the ground, tail

still dangling in the water. She sings into Jarek's ear, using her siren's voice.

Troy turns to look at me, afraid to say anything and risk my cousin hearing us. I pull him under the water to keep our voices from echoing.

"She said they would be together, one way or the other," I whisper. "Troy, I think she's sirening him."

"That's not how we're supposed to use those abilities," Troy counters.

"I know." I glance at my cousin's blue tail, the ends of her long, dark locks floating in the water around her waist. "I don't think Jarek is actually in love with her like she says he is, Troy."

"I don't think so either."

Jarek leans forward, laying down on his stomach to be closer to Persephone. He looks mesmerized by her voice as he leans toward her.

She reaches up, entangling her hand in his. Slowly, she dips their hands into the cool water, bringing it back up a moment later. Seph leans forward singing in his ear a mere inch away.

When she looks toward the water, he smiles at her. Jarek pushes forward, diving into the water while still holding her hand.

Troy and I immediately back up, shooting under the water toward the cavern entrance. We hide behind the walls, only allowing our eyes to peek beyond the rocks.

Jarek and Persephone remain under the surface, bubbles slipping up to where the water meets the air. When she doesn't pull the prince up, I begin to panic. Even Troy grabs a hold of me, worry evident in his nervous fingertips.

Persephone places her lips on Jarek's, breaking them apart for a kiss. She kisses him over and over as the remaining air in the prince's lungs slips away.

"She thinks her love will help him breathe underwater," I murmur, thinking back to what my cousin had said earlier.

"She's not *magic*!" Troy cries. "We have to do something."

"She's going to kill him," I realize, snapping out of the fog I was in, coming back to my senses.

I dart forward, racing through the water toward the pair. Troy immediately follows, quickly overtaking me with his powerful tail. I silently curse the pearls around my torso for slowing me down.

Troy rips them apart just as I reach them. My hands grasp Seph's shoulders as I wrench her back in the water. Shocked, she doesn't fight me for a moment.

When she does come back to life, it's too late—Troy is already carrying Jarek to the surface. With an incredible show of strength, Troy lifts the man onto the land as my cousin lashes out at me.

I slap, twisting her around and letting go before

darting to the surface quickly enough that I propel myself out of the water like a dolphin or a whale and land alongside of Jarek's lifeless body.

"Handle him," Troy directs me, turning back to keep my cousin away while I work.

Once, when I was younger, I watched a child toddle into the ocean. His distracted tutor reached him long before I did and when I reached the shore, the man was pressing on the child's chest, trying to expel the water from his body. Miraculously, the child came back to life.

I throw my weight against Jarek's chest, though I don't have the leverage I need from a sitting position—I supposed that's at least *one* use for having legs. I beat against him the way the tutor viciously fought against death for the small boy.

After minutes—or a lifetime—Jarek coughs up water. He chokes as he sits up.

"It didn't work," he says sadly.

"What were you thinking?" I chastise him. "You nearly died, Jarek."

"She said it would work."

"Well, it didn't!" I can't help my exasperation. "That was foolish and careless. What would your mother do if you died? What would she do if you just *left and lived under the sea*? Jarek, you can't do things like this."

"But I love her," he protests.

"No, you don't. She sirened you. Her singing convinced you to do something you wouldn't ordinarily do—our voices have the power to change minds and fates."

"I don't believe that." He tries crossing his arms, only to trigger another coughing fit.

"Lay back down," I direct him.

"I don't want to," he says stubbornly.

"*Good.* Now pay attention." I start singing, letting my siren-call free. After a moment, he leans back, lying against the cold, harsh rocks of the cavern floor. "Let me remind you that only a moment ago, you refused to lay down, and yet, here you are—laying down.

"It's because I *sirened* you, Jarek," I conclude.

"This is madness," he says, eyes shifting to look at me while he remains on the cavern floor.

"I told you."

Troy and Persephone pop out of the water, breaking the surface loudly as they struggle. I slip into the water.

"Go inside, Jarek. Don't come back to this cavern—ever. I'll come back to you when it's safe, but for coral's sake, don't go near the water alone until I can talk some sense into her."

Jarek looks bewildered as he stares at the mermaid and merman struggling near the mouth of the cavern. They fight like two fish thrown in a bucket, struggling to survive. Their splashing creates large waves that rock me in the water, slamming my stomach into the side of the rocks.

"Jarek, please," I beg for his attention. He tears his eyes off them and focuses on me. "If you go near her and she sirens you again, you could drown—she nearly killed you this time. Please, Jarek, I beg you—don't go near the water alone."

I pull my hands away from the side of the ledge.

"I'll be back. Just go!"

Jarek stands, rushing away from the cavern. I turn, diving under the water toward my cousin, fury running through my veins.

I catch her by the tail and drag her away from the cavern—my strength surprising even me. She tries to pull away, but it only serves to jerk my arm back and forth as I move her backward under the waves. Troy catches up to me, wrapping his hand around her tail just above mine, lending me his strength should I need it to pull her.

Persephone screams the entire way to the seafloor, but we don't stop until we reach the coral that surrounds the land kingdom, indicating where the swimmers should turn around.

"What were you thinking?" I scream at my cousin. "You drowned him! He *died*, Persephone!"

"He didn't," she counters, still trying to pull away from us. "He would have breathed, I know it."

"No, he wouldn't have. He's a *human*—he's not made

to live under the water."

"Persephone, you're playing a very dangerous game here," Troy warns her. "Your grandfather would never approve."

"He understands *love,*" she growls at us, looking like a shark that has spotted its prey.

"I've had enough." I latch on to her wrist. Troy immediately matches me, turning Seph around in the water to swim the same way we are. We force her along. She bucks like an eel, trying to slither away from us.

When we arrive, the festivities are in full splash. Mer fill the waterways, adorned in pearls and fancy *iluses,* belts, chestplates and shoulder armor.

We go immediately to the palace where we find Persephone's mother.

"What is going on here?" she looks horrified at us, pulling her daughter along as if we are a jellyfish pulling its dinner toward itself.

"She tried to drown Prince Jarek," I announce indignantly.

"Excuse me?" my aunt snorts.

"She sirened him because she's in love with him and he drowned. I barely managed to save him."

"I did no such thing," Persephone protests, struggling against us. Her tail crashes into mine and I worry I might have lost a few scales.

My aunt swims to us, grabbing her daughter's hand

away from Troy. She turns, dragging Seph behind her, locking them in her daughter's room.

"Go get my grandfather," I turn to Troy. "I'll wait here."

I set up vigil outside my cousin's door. I can't make out what my aunt and Persephone are saying, but it sounds harsh. I feel terrible that my cousin is suffering, but it's better to get it over with now before it becomes harder to handle—and more dangerous.

"Gather your cousins," Grandfather says after I explain the situation. "We'll talk in the grotto."

I suddenly wish Troy had been able to stay by my side through the lecture, but only the cousins were allowed to participate in the discussion. Our parents hovered near the rocky walls while the younger generation floats closer to our patriarch.

Persephone's mother argues with Grandfather, raging about Persephone's right to siren a man she loves—I hadn't anticipated her taking her daughter's side.

"We were not meant to use our gifts to hurt others, daughter," Grandfather says dangerously. His tail flicks behind him, showing his rage. "Our songs are only meant

"Aila"
by Madeline Elwood

to help and guide. We have always used our voices to protect."

"We all understand our duty and agreement to help the humans," my aunt snaps. "We've all honored that. It's nearly a rite of passage for mer to guide a ship through a storm or locate and rescue a drowning human."

She places her hands on her hips, glaring.

"Mer have done a great deal for the humans—*more than they've done for us*—and there is no reason to take this from Persephone."

Persephone weeps near the side of the room. My cousins all keep their distance until they decide if it's safe to associate with her or not in front of Grandfather.

"She will never have any place here. Your title will be passed to your eldest, and then to her eldest." My aunt glares at my older cousin, Kailania. "Persephone could have her own title and kingdom and it wouldn't affect anyone here—in fact, it would only make the human-mer bond stronger."

"How do you expect her to live like that—her in the sea and him on land—what kind of a *life* is that?" my grandfather challenges. He turns on Persephone. "You will not see the prince again. You both were made for so much more. It may not be fair, but it is the way that it is."

"Father!" my aunt shouts.

"This violates the human-mer agreement. We've honored it for one hundred years, daughter," my grandfather rages, voice filling the grotto. "Do you remember what happened when humans first discovered merpeople? They captured the mer in their nets and strung their bodies up on their ships, taking them back to land as trophies, even giving their corpses as rewards. Marcelline had to risk her life to go to the humans, convincing them that we were more valuable as an alliance than an enemy —she saved our people from certain death as the humans made it their mission to pull us from the sea."

"And if you'll recall," my aunt sneers, "that started with sireny too—that's how Marcelline convinced them to sign the agreement. It wasn't by her wonderful words or brilliant strategy. She failed to convince the king not to destroy us, so she sang to him and changed his mind."

"And we haven't used our sireny on humans since for anything other than to protect them out on the seas," Grandfather concludes. "Marcelline may not have put it in the agreement with King Leon, but it was always a part of the mer's promise—we would not harm them."

"*The tides are changing,* Father."

"Not as long as I reign," he bellows. "You will follow my orders."

Persephone cries out, racing out of the grotto. Grandfather's nostrils flare as he motions to one of my uncles by the door.

"Follow her," he turns on my aunt, anger burning in his eyes. "*You* will stay."

Several of the uncles follow Persephone out. The rest of us hover in place, afraid to move. The arguing continues for several hours.

I finally sink to the floor, leaning against the walls as the parents fight with Grandfather and my aunt, Chantay. I'm surprised at which side some of them take. My cousins and I listen quietly.

My fingers float up, dancing in a school of tiny fish absent-mindedly when the uncles race back in. They look frantic as they fill the room.

"Persephone went to the surface," one proclaims.

"She went to the prince. His mother was there—" another adds.

"She tried to siren him from the shores and when he ran to the water, the queen's men stopped him."

"Barely," my eldest uncle mumbles.

"The queen and her guards rushed to the water, while her men held back the prince," my father exclaimed. "Persephone challenged her wishes and refused to leave without the prince.

"When she moved to the shore and sirened him again, the queen had her shackled to the land and demanded we bring you to her."

My aunt races out of the room, not staying to hear more. Grandfather starts to follow but holds back long enough to hear the rest of the information from my uncles on the situation.

He commands us to wait as he swims off with my parents, aunts and uncles to rescue Persephone and make peace with the queen and her son.

The next few hours are the hardest of my life.

"It will be okay," Troy tries to soothe me, combing my hair.

My shell crown sits on the table next to us as he pulls a bone comb through my silver locks. I lean back into his skilled hands as he works his magic on my hair.

In the corner of the room, an octopus sits, watching the scene. I've always been fond of the pink thing that lurks in the palace, though I could do without the occasional brush of its tentacle.

"I'm sure they'll be back soon," Kailania remarks for the tenth time. Her fingers slip nervously to her crown adorned in gems and crystals. Pearls accent each rock for the festivities.

"This is a fabulous way to celebrate the opening ceremonies," one of the girls mumbles.

"Should we take over with the parade?" I ask, realizing that no one has been overseeing the events.

"I'll go if they aren't back soon," Kailania says in a

confident voice. She may not be strong-willed, but when it comes to her royal duties, she holds true.

Troy's movements are comforting. One of my cousins eyes him with jealousy. Several of our companions occupy the room with us, though none of the newer relationships are welcome yet until we get to know them. Troy is particularly good-looking compared to the others, despite them being some of the most eligible mermen in the kingdom.

"Did you find her?" Kailania asks, swimming up quickly from her seat.

One of my uncles cradles his arm in his hand. My mother looks worse for the wear. My youngest aunt—the peacemaker—has a nasty scratch across her cheek.

"We found her," Grandfather confirms. "I convinced the queen to leave Persephone in my custody and we had planned on discussing how to handle the situation."

He pauses, deciding how to continue.

"Send the messengers," he turns to my uncles. "Send them into every kingdom under the sea—no one is to surface until this is resolved.

"The mer are not to leave the depths, or they risk their lives and our treaty and future safety."

Something terrible has happened.

"Grandfather?" I push away from my seat, nearly knocking Troy's hand away.

"Your aunt made a terrible decision," my grandfather

says, voice laced in sadness. "When the queen wouldn't relinquish Persephone to anyone but me, your aunt swam away. The queen thought it was to find me and bring me to the surface faster, but instead, she swam to the coves where the fisherman like to work."

I hold my breath, already knowing where this was going. Squeezing my eyes shut, I mourn the loss of my friend and our lives as we know them.

"She sirened a ship, luring them onto the rocks. The men all drowned and the ship was lost." He hangs his head in shame. "She broke the treaty and now we're all in danger.

"Everyone must stay under the sea until I can fix this with the queen."

"The people," my uncle interjects, "are angry. They already know what has happened. Many of them are hunting us in revenge."

Just like that, all of Marcelline's work has been undone.

"Gather everyone. The festivities are hereby canceled. I need to address the people and tell them what has happened." Grandfather motions for his children to set everything up for the announcement. "There's something else you should know.

"Before word of the sunken ship reached the palace, your aunt arrived. She took Persephone, claiming she was bringing her home while I tried to calm the queen.

"Several of us went with them to see that they made it back safely, but they attacked us. We don't know where Chantay or Persephone are, nor what they plan to do."

That would explain my mother's appearance.

Grandfather motions us forward, and we follow him to the courtyard to address the people.

At first, everyone sides with my aunt and Persephone, horrified over the thought of one of us being shackled to land. My grandfather calms them down, explaining it was both Persephone and Chantay who were in the wrong for breaking the agreement—the queen's actions, while harsh, were only done to prevent my cousin from doing any more damage until our leader could address the situation.

Grandfather pleaded with everyone to stay inside the festival limits for the time being, urging them that it was safer when we were closer together. Eventually, we all wandered back to where we would spend the night.

"I have something to show you," Troy smirks, tugging at my wrist.

"It's late, Troy," I gently pull back.

"All the better," he teases, swimming away from me. "Coming?"

I sigh, following after him. Kailania and Ebba follow after their mermen as well, working together to get us out of our heads. The mermen guide us away from the palace, into the dark waters.

Several midwater squids join us, illuminating our path with their glowing bodies.

"Where are we going?" I ask.

"To the Scur Caverns," he grins. We all start to swim faster at the thought of the glowing underwater cave that mimics the storm clouds above the surface. It's a beautiful, adventurous location that isn't easy to reach—romantic too.

In the distance, something glows. It's muted and dull, but it's there. Knowing we need to investigate, we veer off course, swimming toward the light as we douse our own, concealing the creatures swimming with us.

Persephone and her mother swim just far enough below the surface that they can't be easily seen by men on ships.

"This can't be good," Troy murmurs.

Kailania dives to the ocean floor, grabbing at the first conch she sees. She whispers into it before attaching it to her squid.

"Home," she commands it. The creature takes off into

the murky waters to deliver her message to our grandfather. "Let's go."

We follow the mermaids toward the land.

"Aila, if it comes to it, you may need to be the one to negotiate with Jarek and the queen—they know you far better than they know me," Kailania says as we race toward them. Catching up to my aunt and cousin seems impossible at this distance.

"It will all be okay," I try to assure her as much as myself. Troy's hand gently finds my waist, lending me his support.

On the surface, guards hold vigil along the water's edge. As we approach, we find them jumping into the sea, drowning.

Persephone and Chantay call to them, ending their lives one at a time until only a few remain. The men run inside, hoping to find reinforcements. Instead, the queen and Jarek run out to investigate.

We reach them just in time to hear Jarek rebuff Persephone's final advances. When he denies her, she sings to him, calling him into her arms.

"No," I scream, trying to break the trance. "Jarek!"

My shrieks are to no avail. Jarek throws himself into the sea, swimming to my cousin. When he reaches her—his mother still screaming from the shore—Persephone drags him under the water.

I dive, the bodies of the dead guards cloud my way

like a bloom of jellyfish. I dart around them, knowing they cannot be saved.

"Let him go, Persephone," I shout, pummeling into her. She keeps her grip.

"They tried to hurt me, Aila. They need to be stopped."

"They shackled you so you wouldn't hurt anyone," I counter.

"The queen would have killed me," Seph shouts.

"Like you're doing to Jarek?" I pull on his arm, desperately trying to free him and take him to the surface for air.

"He turned on me," my cousin informs me.

"And you're turning on everyone. Seph, this is ridiculous!" I cry. "You broke the treaty. It will be a miracle if we can repair the damage you've caused."

"We don't need to repair anything," she informs me, trying to take Jarek deeper into the water. "We won't need to worry about the humans at all—they'll obey our every command."

"We're not going to siren them," I argue. "We've had an agreement for one hundred years—"

"Yes, and now our oppression is over," she looks at me with wild eyes.

I've had enough.

I scratch at her, drawing blood. In the dark of night in the shallow depths of the water near the palace, predators will surely be nearby. She has two choices—sacrifice herself and take the prince down with her, or release him and survive.

Ebba appears next to me, scratching at Persephone as she attempts to pull her away. Seph loses her grip on the prince and I drag him up.

We burst through the surface, the cool night air stinging my cheeks. Ebba pops out of the water, grabbing Jarek's other arm. We pull him toward the shore.

Kailania shouts with the queen, trying to calm her, but with her son out of her sight, the queen's fear turns to rage. Troy and the others try to help, searching the sinking bodies for possible survivors—though we all know there are none. The mermen drag the bodies to the shore to give their families some comfort.

The moon sparkles off the surface of the water. It would have been even lovelier had the water not been so choppy from the rescue efforts. The pale silver glow matches my hair as I force Jarek's lifeless body toward the shore.

"Is he dead?" Ebba asks, panic seething out through her words.

"I don't know," I respond, unsure if he can be saved a second time.

Kailania screams in terror, splashing back in the water.

"Harpoons, get down," she warns us, diving under

the water.

"Go," I command Ebba. She hesitates before diving under the water.

With only a few feet to go, I push my tail with all of the strength I have. I feel like everything in me is going to break. I push Jarek up, slamming his chest into the land.

I can't push him up any higher, so I stabilize him before leaping up to sit on the steps. Pulling does little good.

"Your majesty," I shriek, trying to get the queen's attention. She notices me, running toward us.

Her men notice too.

A harpoon flies in my direction, sinking into the water a few feet away.

"Don't hit Jarek," the queen wails, lifting her skirt to run. She trips, stumbling in the darkness.

Another weapon flies at me—this one dangerously close.

A guard runs at me, overtaking the queen. My eyes grow wide for he has no intention of doing anything other then skewering the mermaid who killed his prince.

"I'm sorry," I whisper to Jarek before throwing myself off the steps I had spent the last few years of my life on.

I knew the moment I touched the water that I would never see those steps again.

"Aila," Troy appears, frightening me. He wraps himself around me, forcing me away from the palace.

Arrows dive into the water, having been shot from the highest towers and walls of Jarek's palace. One slices into Troy's arm, ripping his flesh open.

I scream, but it only pushes Troy to move faster, propelling us away from harm. My hair floats straight out behind me, and I can feel it resisting against the water, slowing us down. I'm suddenly grateful I replaced my pearl *iluse* for a more practical one.

I glance back over my shoulder as Troy guides me. The arrows sink in the distance until we're far enough away that I can't make out their skinny figures in the depths.

"Are you okay?" I croak out, trying to see Troy's injury.

"I'm fine," he replies quickly, out of breath. "Are you hurt?"

"I don't think so," I try to examine myself, but our speed and my adrenaline prevent me from taking a proper assessment.

"Where are Chantay and Persephone?" Kailania asks, her beau wrapped around her waist.

"I don't know," I reply as Troy finally slows.

"We need to find grandfather," Ebba insists, swimming back toward us—her merman clearly having pulled her away before Kailania and I escaped. I am grateful to him for protecting her when we couldn't.

"Did Jarek live?" Kailania inquires. She looks as

"Aila"
by Millenium Genesis

though her own life were the one in question.

"I don't know," I can feel the tears stinging my eyes. "I had to leave him."

Kailania nods, her moves deep and heavy.

"This changes everything," she reminds us.

"Girls," grandfather's voice carries to us as he shouts.

We all spin toward the noise, beating our tails against the water to reach him faster. We crash into him at the same time, knocking him back. He waits for us to explain everything. A collection of mer surround us, floating in the water with the glowing squids.

"I have to go," Grandfather murmurs, pulling us off of him as we protest. "I have to try to fix this."

He takes several of his most fierce mermen with him, swimming for the queen's palace to investigate and try to open a dialogue with the humans.

I fear for his safety.

The depths are quiet as we wait for grandfather to return home.

Light sparkles off the floor of the living quarters, filtering in from the hole in the ceiling. It dances in waves as I focus on it, trying to relieve my worry.

A turtle silently slips into the room, hovering over our

heads as he explores. It turns, exposing its belly to me as it glides across the space over my head.

Jarek once told me the only creatures allowed inside his palace were dogs and cats, though sometimes mice got in. Everything else—like the majestic horse I saw him riding once—lived outside.

To me, that seems so strange, as all of our creatures are free to roam where they like. Fish and seahorses frequent the palace. Starfish take up residence in almost every corner. While larger creatures, like sharks and whales can't get in, even the occasional curious dolphin makes an appearance outside my room.

"He's alive," I murmur. "He has to be."

"What?" Ebba asks, pulling her head from my shoulder.

"Nothing," I turn, stroking her hair. "I was just mumbling."

"You think grandfather is all right, don't you?" she asks, allowing herself to float up several inches.

"I'm sure he's fine," I assure her. She puts her head back on my shoulder.

Another hour passes before Grandfather returns.

"The prince is alive," he informs us. I shudder, astonished that he lived a second time. "We, however, cannot stay here.

"The humans are bent on revenge. We cannot hand

Persephone and Chantay over to them, and now their sailors are coming after us with a vengeance.

"I don't know where Chantay and Persephone are, but we will protect them from the humans' wrath. We will not hand them over.

"Now, we must protect the rest of our community."

"For many years we've had outliers in the mer community," he begins. "Some have chosen to forgo the ways of the mer, turning to sireny and mercilessness to get what they wanted.

"Those mer were found and dealt with," he continues. "It is with heavy heart that I must inform you that today, my own daughter and granddaughter have chosen to take everything away from the mer community.

"The human prince is alive—barely—thanks to Princess Aila," he motions to me as I hang my head. I'm so grateful that my friend is alive, but I know I shall never see him again. "The treaty protecting humans and mer has been broken.

"With this shattering of the agreement our ancestors made one hundred years ago, our ties to the human world have been dissolved," he looks out at the crowd. "We must leave this place and never return."

The crowd's murmur rises up—fear, agony, remorse, and anger enveloping the collection.

"It is no longer safe," my grandfather insists. "While they have never been to our kingdom, they know enough to find it when the time is right. We cannot stay."

The crowd shifts, unsure of how to respond to this sentence.

"I know some of you are against the outlaw of sireny in any case except when it is necessary for survival. For those of you who take that stand, there is no room in this community for you.

"Get your things and leave immediately," he concludes. "There is no place for you with us in the new kingdom district.

"If you insist on living this way, we wish you all the best and pray that you survive the humans' wrath when they discover you. From this day forward, we will no longer accept you as one of our own, nor will we be there to support you in your time of need.

"Make up your mind now, for if you leave, you will never be welcomed into the community again, and if you stay, you will live under our laws for the rest of your days."

A group of mer cautiously rises up, turning their backs on our people—more than I expected. They form a collection at the back of the group before swimming away to collect their things and move on.

"From this day forward, we will live quietly in the depths. We will avoid humans at all costs. Sireny is only to be used in extreme cases of survival and any *intentional* interaction with the humans is punishable. You do not want to suffer those consequences—they may be as extreme as refusing you access to our people if you put us in danger."

He finishes with a speech full of encouraging words, giving the merpeople hope, despite the circumstances. Even I—having lost my best friend, my home, and nearly my life—feel ready to move forward and take the next stroke toward the future.

Grandfather finds me in my room as I'm packing my things for the journey. He knocks gently before swimming in.

"Don't get any ideas about going back to the surface, Aila," he cautions me. "Even if you go, Jarek will never be by the sea again—his mother has moved him to another palace somewhere on land for his safety."

"I wouldn't, Grandfather. I know it isn't safe."

I place my crowns in a chest, packing my *iluses* around them for protection during the move. My fingers fall over a strand of pearls I had planned on wearing for tonight's concert.

He notices me lingering on the piece.

"We'll bring all of our traditions with us, my Aila," he says, placing a hand on my shoulder. He runs a finger through my hair, trying to comfort me.

"You've never been to the palace in Scylla before. I think you'll like it there—it has even better lighting than this place," he offers. It was hard to picture somewhere more magical than my childhood home. "You know I just want you to be safe."

"Of course, Grandfather," I fly to his defense. "You're doing the right thing."

"I'm sorry you got dragged into this mess, Aila. It wasn't fair for Persephone and Chantay to put us in this position."

"No, it wasn't" I reply sadly, turning back to my packing. "We'll be okay."

I scoop up my pile of conch shells that I kept with messages from my parents, friends, and Troy, and place them in my trunk. Grandfather eyes my crowns.

"That one was always my favorite on you," he points to the gold and coral colored crown, encrusted with shells and crystals. "It matches your tail so perfectly."

He sighs.

"We didn't get close to the palace, Aila. We tried, but we found several conch shells the queen left us on the way—that's how we knew what was happening," he waits a moment. "I tried. I'm so sorry."

He swims away, leaving me to finish collecting my things.

The Scylla palace is everything grandfather promised and more—even the water is warmer. A bloom of jellyfish decorates every room and grotto inside the palace walls.

A giant starfish the size of my forearm sits in the corner of my room when I arrive. An octopus scurries off my bed, clearly unhappy with the intrusion.

Several mermen help bring in my trunks, setting them on the sand. I quickly unpack, wanting to use my first day to explore with Troy.

"Princess," one of the mermen says at my door, carrying in a small box for me. "Princess Kailania requested you join her in the grotto."

I close my treasure chests, covering up my crowns and *iluses* as I thank him. Swimming through the palace, I duck around corners until I locate the grotto—it will take a few days to get used to the layout of the palace.

Kailania looks up as I enter, worry clouding her eyes —I wasn't expecting this expression.

"What?"

Grandfather swims out of the corner of the room, holding his hand open to me. A conch shell sits in his palm.

"This was delivered for you," he holds it out to me. "It's from Persephone."

I swallow, terrified to take the shell and listen to her message. Perhaps she is sorry and wants to come to the palace. Maybe she is inquiring about Jarek's well-being and thinks that because of our friendship, I will have an answer and be willing to share it with her.

I lift the shell to my ear, closing my eyes as the sound swirls around the inside of the shell.

"I know what you did," she hisses through the shell. "I know you sabotaged me—you sirened him first. I understand it all now."

I want to pull the shell from my ear but I know I only get to hear the message once.

"You will pay for what you've done to me and my mother, Aila. You stole the man I loved, banished me from my rightful place with our family, and turned me into a villain.

"You will never be safe, Aila. The world has turned against you and so have I. You should be terrified of the humans, but you should be more worried about me—I'm the greatest siren the world has ever seen—I proved that when I sirened Jarek away from you after you cast your song on him—and I will turn the human world against *you* if it's the last thing I do."

Her words die off, fading into sea foam fizzling on the sand.

My family's faces pale when I tell them of my cousin's words.

"She plans to turn the humans against us even more than she already has," my grandfather whispers in disbelief. "How did I go so wrong?"

"I'm sure Chantay is in on this," my mother mutters, flicking her hand to wave off a small school of fish swimming in her direction. They scatter at her movement.

"We need to protect Aila," Grandfather says. A jolt of electricity runs through me as if I had accidentally brushed against a jellyfish when the thought hits me.

"Troy!"

They all look at me.

"I took Jarek from her—" I don't even finish my sentence before the uncles are swimming away to find him for me.

I wait impatiently as they search for him. It takes longer than normal because they have to locate where his family once lived in Scylla.

"He will be okay, I'm sure of it." Kailania brushes her fingers through my hair quickly. Her frantic movements might suggest otherwise.

"Ships have been spotted in areas the humans have

always stayed out of," one of my aunts announces, swimming into the room. "The scouts are back and it doesn't look good."

I'm positive it will be another hundred years before my kind sees the surface again.

"Aila," Troy rushes to me, ignoring the rest of the room. He throws his arms around me, pulling me close. "What happened?"

I quickly explain Persephone's threats, earning myself a look of horror. He spins us around to face my family.

"She will be protected," Grandfather cuts him off. "I understand your worry, my boy, but she will be under the best care possible."

"We'll be baiting the sharks, surrounding the easiest places to enter the kingdom. We'll teach them where to hunt so that they also protect us," my mother explains, clearly having thought this through. "They won't leave an area with an easy food source—we'll provide them with enough motivation to stay, and no one will want to face them to get to us."

"The other entryways are harder to access. It won't be easy for anyone—mer or human—to reach us here once we're done," Grandfather concludes. "And the coral reefs will do the rest."

Grandfather sends mer to see to the sharks, putting their plan into action immediately. We spend the rest of the day working on a plan to keep me safe and unpack the palace.

That night, Troy insists on sleeping outside my door.

Troy leaves early the next morning, long before the cuddlefish have gone to bed for the morning. I comb my hair, not knowing what else to do now that I'm on restriction.

"Princess," a merman hovers in front of my door. "A conch was delivered for you. It's from Princess Ebba."

Conch shells whisper the name of the recipient until it is delivered, but the sender's voice can often be identified if the person who finds it has met them before.

"I'm trapped," Ebba cries. "I'm in a cavern."

She quickly details the location, begging for help.

"Aila, it's Persephone—she says to come alone or she'll take my fins." Ebba sobs into the conch shell. Without her fins, she can't swim—it's one of the worst fates a mermaid can suffer.

Sneaking out of the palace takes a tremendous amount of work. Thankfully, a giant sea turtle glides by the palace walls just as I peek around the corner. I hide behind its shell as it swims away, blocking me from view of the mer guards outside my new home.

When I finally depart from my slow-moving ride, I swim as quickly as I dare toward the location Ebba described. Finding my way around in new surroundings isn't easy, but I quickly discover that Persephone has left signs for me along the way.

She waits outside the cavern with Ebba, her hands tied behind her back. Several strands of seaweed cover Ebba's mouth, preventing her from calling out to me.

Next to her rests a long chain extending to the surface —an anchor.

"We've been inside waiting for you this whole time," Persephone informs me, a sharp shell knife to Ebba's throat. She darts her gaze up to avoid removing her hands from their control over the pink-haired girl. "They're looking for us."

"I'm here, Seph. Let Ebba go."

She pushes our cousin back toward the cavern.

"Now be a good mermaid and stay put. Someone will be along to help you in a bit." She pats Ebba on the head. Obviously, she still cares about her, but she's also willing to use her to hurt me.

Persephone guides Ebba into the cavern as I swim close. A moment passes with no movement.

"Can't we just talk about this?" I beg, steering clear of the metal weight holding the boat at bay.

"No," she yells, launching herself out of the dark mouth of the cave.

In her hands, she holds a net. Not realizing it was coming, I didn't have time to move. My hands work quickly to rip it off of my body, tail trashing to set myself free.

"They want a mermaid head—any head will do. Those men up there are looking for me, but they don't know the difference between one mermaid and another. I watched them gut a fish half your size and throw it back in the water almost a league from here."

"Persephone!" I struggle against my captor as she pushes me to the ocean floor.

"Actually, you have good timing," she says, pointing up. "Here comes their net."

Once it settles in the water, she drags me up. I try swimming away, but my tail is so constricted by the net, that I can barely move, much less escape.

We're mere inches from the fishermen's net when I find myself floating, falling away from near-capture. Kailania wrestles with Persephone above me in the water.

The moment I hit the ocean floor, I wriggle myself around, trying to get the net undone. Miraculously, a shell lies on the seafloor.

I beat it against the sand, but it doesn't break. My last resort is snapping it with my hands. I push so hard, I think I might break every bone in my fingers before the shell will snap.

Kailania is pushed dangerously close to the net above

me. With a final snap, I break the shell in two, slicing my hand open in the process. It stings as I use the jagged edge of the shell to cut the ropes around me just enough to escape.

My eldest cousin tips Persephone into the net as she tries to swing herself away from it just as the net starts to rise out of the water. Persephone's face is pure terror as she screams for help.

Kailania freezes, processing what is happening. We're banned from helping the mer that left the community… but she's also our dear cousin, and no matter what she has done, we love her.

"Aila!" Kailania screams as I dart back to the ocean floor.

I scoop up the broken shell pieces and race as quickly as I can to the net entrapping Persephone, my own net over my arm. I pass off one half of the broken shell, transferring the net to my non-dominant arm as I saw at the ropes.

"Faster," I warn Kailania. Glancing up, I can see we only have seconds left to spare my cousin from certain death.

The moment she is free, Persephone tries to escape. Kailania brings her shell down on Seph's temple, knocking her out. She sinks quietly to the ocean floor

"Get her in the net," Kailania murmurs, racing toward the sandy bottom of our kingdom.

We tie her up. I float over her as my older cousin rushes into the cavern to get Ebba—she hadn't realized the girl was there when she rescued me.

Kailania had heard from the man who delivered the conch to me that I had received a shell message from Ebba. When she couldn't locate either of us, she figured out what had happened and had come after me. She spotted me from the palace just as I separated from the giant sea turtle and had trailed me the entire way.

Ebba had been knocked out the moment Persephone had pushed her into the cave, but she woke up long before Seph did. Together, the three of us dragged Persephone back to the palace.

Half of the kingdom is looking for us by the time we return. The mermen take Persephone's bucking body from us, carrying her netting back to the palace.

"Granddaughter, you will answer for your crimes. You will never again leave this palace. Take her to the cells." Our grandfather makes a sweeping motion, summoning his mermen to take her away. "You are my granddaughter, so we will show you mercy, but you will never again see the outside of your cell. *I so proclaim it.*"

"What will we do about Aunt Chantay, Grandfather?"

Kailania asks, swimming across the room once Persephone has been taken away.

"I fear we will never find her, nor will she stop trying to get to Persephone.

"You are safe, my dear ones," he looks around at us. "I promise you that. Chantay will not be able to enter our kingdom, but I cannot stop her from trying to destroy the human world and perpetuate the problem between human and mer."

He looks striking as the light filters down from the ceiling, bits of sand floating in the water like stars in the night sky about the surface. His shoulder armor adds a fierce touch to his presence. I have every confidence that my grandfather will protect us.

"The war, my dears, *has just begun.*"

CONTINUE THE STORY

Origins of The Siren Wars
is the prequel novella to The Siren Wars Saga.

You can continue the story by visiting
sirenwarsinfo.kmrobinsonbooks.com

About K.M. Robinson

K.M. Robinson is a storyteller who creates new worlds both in her writing and in her fine arts conceptual photography. She is a marketing, branding and social media strategy educator who is recognized at first sight by her very long hair. She is a creative who focuses on photography, videography, couture dress making, and writing to express the stories she needs to tell. She almost always has a camera within reach. Visit her at her website for free books and exclusive samples: www.kmrobinsonbooks.com

CONNECT ON SOCIAL MEDIA

facebook.com/kmrobinsonbooks

instagram.com/kmrobinsonbooks

twitter.com/kmrobinsonbooks

youtube.kmrobinsonbooks.com

Get free books and excerpts of other K.M. Robinson books at excerpt.kmrobinsonbooks.com

ALSO BY K.M. ROBINSON

The Jaded Duology

Book One: Jaded

Book Two: Risen

The Golden Trilogy

Book One: Golden

Forged: A Golden Novella

Book Two: Locked

Book Three: Edge

The Legends Chronicles

Along Came A Spider: A Prequel Novelette

And They'll Come Home: A Prequel Novelette

Virtually Sleeping Beauty: A Novella Retelling

The Siren Wars Saga

Book One: The Siren Wars

Book Two: Darker Depths (Coming June 2018)

Book Three: Beyond The Shores (Coming July 2018)

The Revolution Of Jack Frost (Coming Nov 2018)

Were it a more meaningful day, Jager of Limnaia wouldn't think twice about prying himself from his bed, but today was nothing special. A change of the season and thus a great deal of the village celebrated. He had no reason to be out of bed.

His brother Kriegen, star pupil of the local coven, thought otherwise, he was up early and he could hear Kriegen rustling around. "Try to be a little louder, will you?" he grumbled.

"Well, if you'd get out of bed it wouldn't be an issue," Kriegen sing-sang his reply. In prior years he had earned his way higher up in the coven and he deserved it. He had been studious and absorbed his Mistress' teaching like a sponge, he also bloomed like a bloody anemone and made his brother look like a simple plankton.

Jager stiffened, he dropped his arm and shot a glare at his older brother who seemed impervious to how much noise he was creating. One swift flick of a deep blue tail and he would be able to knock him to the wall, but it wasn't worth the effort.

"It's much too early to be awake, why in the depths are you even awake at this hour?" He scrubbed at his eyes and sat up, tossing the covers aside.

Kriegen shot him a look and shrugged a shoulder. His hair a deep shade of blue, matched his tail. "Someone woke up on the wrong side of the bed today."

A scowl marred Jager's features as he rolled himself out of bed. Today was about praising the god of the sea, Muir. Villagers and Cityfolk alike gave praise to the god, paid tribute and generally wasted their time, at least he thought so.

He believed in the god enough, but he lacked the faith to praise Muir and preferred sleep to the harvesting of crops only to be sent away on the current.

"I woke up just fine." Jager plucked a kelp woven shirt from his wardrobe and pulled it over his head. Unlike Kriegen, his hair was black but it held a blue sheen to it, their tails were nearly identical except for a cluster of emerald-colored scales that hovered just below his belly button.

Kriegen yanked a shirt over his head and raked his fingers through his hair, his sharp blue eyes honed in on his brother. "You would do well to respect our god," he cautioned his brother.

"I admire you looking out for me and all, but I assure you I respect Muir well enough." In truth, Jager did little praising or worshipping, the brothers didn't exactly share the same views. While he was more relaxed in his beliefs, his brother was devout and perhaps that was why he had been gifted with more magic. At the end of the day, Jager didn't really care either way.

Kriegen said no more and spun around in the water, bubbles churned up as he snorted and fled the room.

A snide remark died on his lips and he mourned the loss of the opportunity. Maybe he shouldn't tease him as he did, but what were little brothers for? A decade separated the two of them, which was nothing when it came to Merfolk and in spite of how they treated each other they were fairly close.

Outside of the family home, as anticipated, the seafloor was bustling with activity. Mer coated strings of kelp in luminescent algae of pinks, blues, and greens, which brought the village to life even more.

In spite of Jager's indifference, the village looked brilliant and he knew it was good for the people, it brought the community together. These festivals might have been a waste of resources, in his opinion, but if it brought them joy then so be it.

A clap to his shoulder jolted him from his thoughts.

"Decided to join the celebration, brother?" Kriegen's lips tilted at the corner as he swam around him.

A scoff came from Jager as he moved forward, shooing a nosy firefly squid away from him; its frills ruffled and it shot itself away. "If you can't beat them, join them," he offered and bent down to pick up a basket of finely spun kelp. What would Muir need with *that*? Jager wondered, would He eat it, fashion it into clothing? Maybe those thoughts were sacrilegious but he didn't seem to care and he shrugged.

"I already hooked up the hippocampus, I figured you'd tag along." Kriegen scooped up his basket, it contained pearls and even some diamonds that had tumbled into the sea from the cliffside.

This did nothing to change his mindset, it was wasteful. Such things could have been used for trade instead of offering to a deaf god. What care did the god of the sea have for treasures?

He sighed in resignation and swam toward the cart. "Let's go to the surface," he muttered in defeat.

The entire Mer kingdom of Selith was lit up in celebration, as they began to ascend to the surface, Jager peered over his shoulder and down below. Blips of neon hues bobbed in the sea water. Some happened to be decorations and others were a life form.

As the Hippocampus lifted them to the surface they sprung out first, their powerful front fins hauling the small cart out with them. They exhaled deeply, salt water spraying from their nostrils as they bobbed along the waves.

Off to the side of the cart, an island blocked the view of the open sea, Kriegen began to murmur praises.

There was never a reason to worry about the Uplanders, or rather humans, there had been an agreement several hundred years ago when they became bolder in their voyages. This place belonged to the Merfolk and it was known throughout to never trespass.

The sound of a breath being drawn in caused the brothers to look to the side. "Greetings, Oinone," Kriegen nodded his head to the older Mer.

A smile lit up her pale face, her bright orange and red hair curled against her temple as well as cheeks. "Greetings, it's a fine day for Giving Thanks," she supplied.

"Well enough," Jager agreed and cast his eyes on the colorful island. The trees were ripe with fruit and the flowers contrasted with green leaves. It was the belief of the Mer that the god of the sea lived here and every year at the same time they paid tribute to the Him.

The Mer would bring their best offering and cast it ashore in baskets, it was a sacred piece of land to them and never to be touched by anyone other than the Merfolk.

"Don't mind Jager, he woke up with his fin bent out of shape today," Kriegen jested. He hoisted up his basket and swam toward the small landing where an assortment of items began to collect.

"I did not," Jager protested.

"Yeah, you did," Kriegen grinned and shrugged off whatever argument was about to ensue. "How are you, Oinone?"

"Good. I'm glad to see you here. I'm also glad that you dragged your brother to the surface, too." The Mermaid's light sea green eyes sparkled with mirth.

A grunt came from Jager but he smirked in spite of himself.

The sound of the sea crashing on the shore of the island was mesmerizing or at least it would have been had there not been more voices collecting in the immediate vicinity. There were more Mer collecting around, lugging their offerings to the shore and muttering their prayers. Colorful baskets with treasures from the poor and rich alike. It was one of the few times that the stuffy nobles of Selith willingly had anything to do with those of Limnaia.

"It is almost time," Oinone announced as she swam toward the shoal.

The island was soon surrounded by a mass of Merfolk, not everyone attended but a great deal did. King Eidir was among his people, his proud torso was clad in gold-plated armor and a jewel-encrusted crown nestled on top of his head. He held a great sword carved from whalebone in his grasp and approached the shoal as close as his massive tail would allow him to.

He lowered the sword to his palm and slit it open before allowing his blood to trickle into the water.

"Muir, our Great One, accept our tributes and bless us. We live to serve you, raise us up, guide us." The King bowed his head and sheathed his sword. Gold vambraces reflected the sun's harsh rays as he spun to face his people.

"Let us rejoice!" he proclaimed and clasped the hand which was closest to him.

Jager just so happened to be closest to the Eidir and bowed his head to him. "Your Majesty," he offered softly.

"May you sing true and persevere," the King said in a gentle voice.

"And you as well."

Once all of the Mer had their hands clasped a hum began to rise amongst all of them and a chorus of song erupted. The island seemed to respond, too, for the leaves grew and the fruit that had not yet ripened became ripe. Whatever life had begun to die off flourished once more and the air around them seemed to still.

The only noise that resounded in the area were the voices of the Merfolk. The sea had calmed and looked as if it were crafted out of glass, the wind had died and the gulls that cried overhead had grown silent.

Just as quickly as it had begun, it ended.

The sea grew lively again and the murmurs of parting between the folk began.

Jager propelled himself from the shoal and spun around to face two approaching figures; Oinone and Kriegen. Oinone was a peculiar mermaid, as far as he knew she had never taken up a spouse and she was known for being eccentric. It went beyond the neon colors she wrapped herself in or how she usually had a red octopus resting in the crook of her arm. It was her views, they were liberal in the highly conservative communities.

"I was just telling your brother that you ought to come back to my place. You may have both graduated recently, but I'll say it… I do miss you, boys. Once a week opposed to hours a day… it's a drastic change. You're akin to children to me." She smiled and swept her wild hair back.

As much as Jager enjoyed Oinone and all her peculiarities, he wasn't often willing to partake in a one on one social event. He often found curt replies coming from his mouth without even meaning it, a personality flaw. Not that Oinone seemed to mind it, however, he could see she preferred Kriegen. He was kind, generous and outgoing.

He looked at his brother and read his expression. A sigh made his shoulder's heave and he nodded his head.

The house happened to be as eccentric as the owner, there were at least five octopi that Jager had counted. Their slitted gaze rolled around in an unnerving way and more than once he felt tentacles wrapping around the base of his tail or tickling the back of his neck.

Red, black, liver. They came in varying shades and as if that wasn't bad enough a few firefly squids scuttled into his view and Jager was forced to clench his fists lest he knocked one of the glowing annoyances out the nearest window.

Onione approached Jager and Kriegen with two cups of tea.

"So, I heard a whisper in the current," she began as she settled into a seat and one of her octopi took up residence on her abdomen. It playfully allowed the tentacles to caress its mistress.

Jager made a face and dipped his head toward the cup to avoid watching.

"And what does the current have to say these days?" Kriegen asked as he took a seat and sipped his tea, relaxing until his back hit the chair.

He had spent far too many days inside this peculiar hut. Bones which were painted in glowing algae hung about and an old assortment of Uplander's utensils littered the area. Vases, mirrors, combs and even an old bureau that seemed to be rotting away.

There were many scavengers that rifled through shipwrecks and pulled the finds from within. Although there was no love for the Uplanders, their items were certainly unique and conversational pieces.

"The humans are growing bolder and it would seem they are beginning to skim our boundaries. It is said they grow greedy and long for new land," she paused and lowered her eyes. "I fear what that means for Noman's Island." She sighed heavily.

If the humans were to trample on their treaty it would change a great deal, for one it would disrupt the

Merfolk's festivals and tributes. For two, it would peg the humans as an enemy. They were known for not keeping their promises, but this one seemed extreme, even for them.

"They cannot have it, it doesn't belong to *them*," snapped Kriegen. At that moment it was clear he was Jager's brother for his face was warped by a scowl.

Jager snorted as if it would stop the humans by simply shouting: This land isn't your land, this land is *my* land.

Oinone patted her hand in the water as if to settle Kriegen, she ignored his brother's indifference. "We are all well aware of that, my darling, but the truth of the matter is it won't stop them. All we can do is be prepared and as the local coven it is our duty in adjacent to the King's Army that we protect our kind and lands."

"And what is it, pray tell, that the Galathea Coven is willing to do to the humans when they shred our agreement?" Jager's voice came out rougher than he intended, his blue eyes sharp on Oinone's smooth face.

Bloodshed wasn't an option, Galathea was known for being peaceful and Selith for all of its haughtiness was not keen on fighting wars. There were other kingdoms in the sea that preferred to bear arms, but Muir knew Selith was full of guppies.

Jager' lips pressed together and when he looked over at Kriegen he noted the stormy look in his gaze. "It's nothing they haven't tried before, Kriegen, they won't succeed."

In return, he received a steely look. His brother sat the cup down and folded his arms across his chest. "They won't take what is ours I won't let them." Kriegen's fingers curled into his flesh as he shook his head.

"Don't trouble yourself now, Kriegen, it will all work out. I have faith. In Muir, in us, and perhaps even the humans," Oinone offered and moved from her seat. A black octopus grumpily tumbled to the floor of the hut, its slitted yellow eyes narrowing at its owner before it blew bubbles in her direction.

Jager watched the creature and shuddered.

"I don't see why you have such faith in humans, it isn't as if they have ever stuck to their word. They once hunted our kind, mounted us on piers like prized fish," Kriegen ranted, his eyes watching as his prior Mistress began to rummage through one of her stone shelves.

"I have an equal amount of faith in everyone, my darling. One can only hope for the best in all things."

"Okay, as much as I enjoy this weighted and positive moral talk I have things to do at home still. Oinone, thanks for the tea." He lifted the cup and set it down on a nearby table.

His brother slowly turned his head toward him and flicked his fingers in the water. "Go home without me, I'll be along soon enough."

Silenced filled the hut and it gnawed at Jager as he swam from the confinement. His brother wasn't the sort to brood or even snap, but the topic of the humans encroaching on their territory had seemed to change that.

Kriegen was the atypical shining pearl of the glittering sea, he was attractive, good-hearted and of a tender nature, to see his jaw hardening and the glint in his eye was more than a touch unsettling.

The days of laughing beside his brother seemed to be gone. Their mother had passed away in childbirth with a sibling that didn't thrive in the first few days, she had been too fragile for the harsh sea. It was the death of their father that seemed to break a part of Jager, though.

A few years ago, Seger had surfaced to meet with an Uplander, towing a basket of goods to trade. He had declared the woman was friendly and in need of items, he provided a means to survive in her world. In trade, she offered items that the Merfolk valued, cloth, vanity items and the like.

It didn't take long for a competitor to follow her and the end result was the death of their father. His corpse placed on display on the pier, locked away in a cage.

Neither of the brothers ever forgot and it seemed it wasn't just Jager who didn't forgive.

Inside of the small family home, Jager inspected the bookshelves which were full of various volumes of the old magic. A sigh escaped from him as his finger caught on a nodule he hadn't noticed before. It was an inconsistency in the shelf that most wouldn't take pause for, but when his adept fingers swiped along they found purchase on a button.

He pushed it and a compartment opened to reveal a book, why in Muir's name would a volume be hidden here? Jager pulled it out and examined it, swallowing roughly when it became clear as to *what* kind of book it was.

With trembling fingers, he quickly shoved it back inside where it had come from. It wasn't just any magic book, but one of the Dark Arts, one that called upon the evils of their magic instead of the light within. As sour as he was in personality, never once had he been tempted to even read a piece of literature that spoke of the dark.

"Why, Kriegen? Why?" Jager whispered in a shaky voice and swam out of the house.

There were chores to tend to, for the family had a small farm prior to the death of both parents. The hippocampus needed to be fed and he was fairly certain land dues were today.

He would address this with his brother when he came home. Or so he told himself.

By the time Kriegen returned home, Jager had already tended to everything. The dues were paid, the livestock fed and cleaned, the house tidied. It was rather amazing what one could do when they were fueled by stress and worry.

Kriegen's gaze swept along the house and he let out a small laugh. "Were you going stir crazy?" He shook his head and swam to the kitchen. The light in his eyes had returned and his disposition seemed altogether more relaxed, a contrast to what his mood had been earlier.

Perhaps Oinone had worked a miracle, talked some sense into him and put his aggravation at ease, but something niggled in the back of Jager's mind and told him otherwise. He bit his tongue and shrugged a shoulder.

"Brother mine, someone has to be a house wench and it certainly isn't you," he teased as he reclined in the chair, his tail flicking up over the arm of it.

A grunt came from Kriegen as he made himself a salad.

"Your mood seems lighter, did Oinone work some

magic on you?" he asked, trying to keep his tone from sounding as if he were digging.

Kriegen turned around with the bowl in his hands and sat at the dining table. "Yeah, something like that," he laughed his words out before he stabbed some of the food with his utensil and piled it into his mouth.

That was good enough for him, at least for now. "I paid the dues and everything else has been taken care of."

"Wow, you *were* a busy sea wench." He winked and waved his fork around.

Oinone certainly did know how to weave magic, Jager mused. He mulled over the idea of the coven's principals, which was to protect their kind and land no matter the cost.

"I'll be going out tonight," Jager offered.

"On a...date?" Kriegen ventured, his brows lifting up.

A laugh erupted from Jager as he floated upward, his tail flicking as he swept his hair away from his eyes. "No." He turned toward the door and rapped his fingers on the wall. "I'm still holding out for *the one*." A smirk formed on his lips.

One last chuckle from his brother and he was swimming off.

It was nice not having to explain where he was going, not that he would have spilled the truth but rather he would have conjured up a lie. There was no need for Kriegen to know where he was off to and he certainly didn't want to stir up trouble.

A mutter escaped from him as he swatted a trouble-some cuttlefish away, the blasted thing swam backward and zipped around the side of him before it allowed its facial tentacles to tickle at his neck.

"Argh! Disgusting," he cried out and shuddered as he batted it away.

The rest of the ascent was quiet, he felt his body expand as he swam from the depths and at last he surfaced. Water spilled down his face and plastered his hair on his shoulders. Beyond the choppy water the Uplander's were busy on their docks, curious, he swam forward and came to rest beneath one of the wooden piers.

"Captain Hook, we are nearly ready to set out on our voyage," one of the crew members spoke up.

"Aye, that is good," the Captain replied.

From what Jager could see between the cracked wooden planks the Captain was young, maybe twenty-three. His black hair was chin length, his clothing of deep black as well as blue and on his hip hung a rapier sword. The hilt of weapon was impressive, it wasn't so much the blade itself but the knuckle bow which was black.

He looked like a pirate.

As the Captain moved onto the ship, Jager spied a redheaded kid who lingered behind.

"...and when we reach the mark I set last time, that will be the time, got it?" His companions nodded their head and before long they were boarding the ship, too.

The commands of the captain rung out and the ship came to life, beginning to rock as if it was all too eager to tear across the open seas. As the crew prepared and fulfilled their tasks, the sails snapped in the wind and the ship began to part from the dockside.

Jager was not a paranoid individual, but he half wondered if this meant that these Uplanders were about to encroach on their territory. If this was the moment or if this was a harmless voyage to gather intel on surroundings islands, perhaps expand their knowledge for cartography reasons.

Or maybe that was just wishful thinking.

A silent sigh left him as he dipped below the waves and dove just low enough in the water so that his figure was not a shadow to the surface. He did what anyone in his position would do, which was follow the ship.

In hindsight, this was a fool's errand and even at the

moment, he knew that. If something were to go awry, say, the crew notice him or decide to dip a net into the water, Jager would be in trouble. Yet, here he was, all he could do was fight to keep up with the ship and remain somewhat below the belly of the beast. That way no one would notice him and the nets stood no chance of capturing him.

As the ship continued to sail, Jager took notice that it was staying well away from the boundaries that were set. They were not staying on the course they wanted because there was, in fact, a ward set in place, one that didn't prohibit the Uplanders from traversing onto Merfolk territory by ship, but one that would make them well aware they broke the treaty. The Coven protected the waters by guarding them and the soldiers took care of them by fighting for them.

Just as he was considering nothing exciting was to happen a body plunged into the sea. A body that had weighted chains wrapped around it and it sunk past him rapidly.

A thought of allowing the human to plunge to their death passed his mind. What had humans ever done for him or his family? They had murdered his father and strung him up on display for everyone to see. Yet, he couldn't allow the blasted human to drown.

Cursing, he swam after the human and caught his body. Dark eyes stared at him in shock.

He didn't speak, but he hummed and allowed magic to break down the metal bindings and they slid away with ease. His fingers dug into the clothing and flesh of the male as he ascended.

The male gasped and sputtered, water spewed from his mouth and nose. "T-T-Thank y-y-you," he stuttered. His eyes blinked rapidly. "M-M-Merma…"

"Mer*man,* stay quiet, what is going on?" he ground his words out.

"Mut-t-tiny," he replied. A distinct stutter made it more difficult for his words to come out.

"What is your name?"

"Smee." The sludge trickled down the male's face and it was now discernable that this wasn't a man but a boy, a teen boy. He couldn't have been much older or younger than Jager for that matter, but his body lacked the definition and fat.

"Mutiny? And then what?"

"P-Peter," the boy sucked in a breath and tried to calm himself the more riled he became the harder it was to speak. "He wants the island that belongs to no man. To c-c-laim it and w-win the favor of the King of Stenf-fisk."

Another body slammed into the sea, but Jager wouldn't be able to keep all of them afloat, as it was he had already taxed himself enough trying to keep up with the ship.

A string of curses left him, Jager pinned a glare on the

golden head above. "Smee, I won't be able to keep you afloat for much longer, just... trust me." What was he saying? There was no other option, he had to stop or at least set the newly appointed captain back for a moment.

Jager lifted a hand and began to sign sigils and a low hum resonated in his chest. The ocean began to respond to him, curling around Smee and dragging him away from the merman. He lifted one hand to silence the teen and pushed his hands forward to control the movement of the sea.

The water lifted him up the length of the ship and toward the skiff attached to the side. His anxious face paled but once he was lowered down and the water pulled back he seemed to relax.

Another body fell into the turbulent sea and this time Jager dove in after them. He did as before and broke the chains away and sent the human, this one aged, with the boy.

"Hook! You should have listened," came the familiar voice Jager heard on the dock. "Do you not want glory? Do you not want the King to look to us with respect, to be honorable?" His tone wasn't gruff, instead, it was exasperated.

"I *am* honorable. I adhere to the treaties, you idiot!" Captain Hook sounded panicked, as he should be.

"They can't own the ocean and an island," scoffed Peter.

"Yes, yes they can. The last time I checked you aren't magically inclined unless you're part fae and kept that from me." Silence spread between them.

Their squabbles allowed for Jager to dip into the depths, his mouth parted as he began to sing the notes that called upon the magic that coursed through his veins. His fingers created the sigils that amplified the magic and soon the water in front of the ship began to spiral.

At first, it was nothing, but then it swelled into a large whirlpool.

"Whirlpool!" a crew member cried out.

Jager didn't stay to find out what happened next, but he ensured that for now, the ship would not be able to trespass into the Merfolk's waters, he needed to buy the time the wards would not provide.

It was time to alert the others. So much for Oinone's faith.

At the seafloor, Jager found two conchs and enchanted them with a message. One for the King to prepare and another to Kriegen to explain what was going on. He magicked each shell and sent them speeding through the water to the intended individual.

Hurriedly, he made his way to Oinone and pounded on her door once before letting himself in. "Oinone!" he shouted breathlessly. His eyes were wild as he looked around for her.

"Oinone!" he bellowed as he swam further into her hut.

"Jager? What is it darling?" She swam out to meet him, concern painted across her face.

"Uplanders… They're attempting to take Noman's…" he puffed his words out and gulped down some water to draw in oxygen. "There was a mutiny and they aim to take the island today. I halted them for now, but we need to stop them."

The Mermaid's green eyes widened and she lifted a hand to her mouth. "Did you send word to the Palace?"

"I did, and to Kriegen," he paused and narrowed his eyes at the look on her face. "What?"

"I don't think that was wise. I have a feeling…" her words trailed off as the door snapped open again.

A huffing Kriegen propelled himself through the door. Whatever laughter returned to his eyes earlier was gone and his blue eyes seemed almost black. His veins on his forearms looked strange, almost blackened.

"Krie.." Jager tilted his head to the side. "You all right?"

Kriegen turned his gaze to his brother and nodded. "I summoned the rest of the coven, let us go wait for them beneath the surface. I assume you sent for the King and his army?"

Jager nodded.

No more was spoken as the three of them left the hut and began to swim toward the surface.

The swim to the surface was a blur, Jager didn't feel the exhaustion he had in the hut thanks to the adrenaline that coursed through him. As he came to the location of the whirlpool everyone spotted the bottom of the massive creation.

Peter had shifted the vessel into the channel to avoid the whirlpool, but because it wasn't of a natural creation and had been brought to life it followed the vessel like a shadow. It drew strength from Jager and eventually it would falter, but his magic was strong. Since the coven would be here soon he didn't worry, they would aid in maintaining it or constructing something stronger.

A body plunged into the water and descended until it was almost level with the collecting coven. There was a wild look in the eyes of the redhead and Jager knew at once it was Peter, the kid was bent on getting to the island.

Noman's Island was sacred, Jager might not have

believed their god still cared but it belonged to *them*.

"You piece of..." A spear sailing by Kriegen cut his words off and the weapon narrowly missed the boy.

Peter began to swim as fast as he could toward the land, he saw the Merfolk and didn't seem surprised. He was bloody stupid!

The boy was daft! There was no point in swimming there, he would never be able to take it, especially surrounded by Merfolk.

A snarl ripped from Kriegen, his hair floated around his body and lashed in the water as if it had a life of its own. "I will not tolerate this!"

No one else was tolerating it either, Jager thought and had the moment not been as severe he would have made light of the situation by pointing it out. However, he feared for their land, but he feared for his brother most.

"Brother, what have you been doing?" he asked softly, but loud enough for him to hear.

There was no reward of a glance but a flick of the tail was given. "We must protect what belongs to us, they are *greedy* and when the mass population discovers the truth of us we will be hunted to extinction - just like our father." The words were hissed as he swam away.

The witches in the area jerked as the wards triggered, they all felt it and soon the entire Kingdom would know what was transpiring. Even the water responded and instead of erupting into violence, it stilled. The whirlpool vanished and the surface looked much like glass.

Renewed with urgency, Jager signed his magic and from it came thick cords of seawater, it was akin to the brine pool past the depths of the Merfolk. Slicing through the water, it snaked around the figure of Peter and since the tendrils were only liquid they couldn't keep a hold on him. However, it could spin and pull him away with a current, which was exactly what it did.

He pulled harder and yanked him back, the blasted redheaded boy kept fighting, clawing and gasping for breath. The thought dawned on him, this could be ended now if he was dragged to the depths and drowned, but Jager wasn't a murderer.

"I wish I *could* damn you to the depths!" he shouted and propelled the teen from the water. A large spout pushed him upward and held him there, it was then that he realized, a little too late, Peter was a distraction.

His blue eyes widened as he saw a flash of white against a backdrop of green. A human was standing on Noman's Island, their sacred ground and tarnishing it with his existence.

A pit formed in Jager's stomach because he knew no good would come of this. They could fight and win today, they could decimate all of the humans and turn their ship into particles of the sea, but would they be the last voyagers that longed to claim what didn't belong to them?

No.

An explosion filled the air, sea spray rained down on the surface and soon after came splinters of wood.

His ears rung, he felt dazed, and when he turned his hand over splinters of wood fell into his hand. It dawned on him that the ship had exploded, Jager's eyes jerked to the scene of the boat that was now up in flames.

A curse left his lips as he ducked beneath the water and propelled himself toward the boat. He could hear the muted cries from above, the sound of the popping fire, and when he surfaced the smell of burning wood assaulted his nose. He coughed as he spun in the water, the smoke was filling the air and the ship still moved toward the island's sandbar.

As Jager blinked his eyes rapidly he realized that it was Kriegen that had caused the explosion, his dark blue hair covered half his face, but even at this distance, the grin was discernible.

"What did you do?" he shouted.

There was a blend of cries, some from the wounded crew and others that had swum to safety on the island. A collection of individuals sat or laid out panting on the shore.

Jager's focus slipped from his brother and toward the struggling blond still suspended in the air by magic. He was laughing in glee and all the merman wanted to do was send him sinking down to rot in the ocean basin.

"You fool! You practically aided them!" he shouted at his brother and curled his fingers into his palm before he yanked his hand to the side. The water that held Peter spun around him and yanked him below the surface before it was released.

Soldiers began to rise to the surface, bone swords in grasp and the coven surrounded the island, too.

"Now we have no choice but to act, Jager, they are on *our* land. They broke a promise and furthermore a treaty," Kriegen stated and flicked back his hair. As he held out his hand a black orb of water formed and he tossed it up as if it were nothing more than a toy to play with.

"No!" Oinone swam over toward Jager and covered her mouth with a hand. "What have you been doing, Kriegen?" her voice came out in a harsh whisper.

His dark blue eyes flickered and he cocked his head to the side. "Trying to protect our people," he replied.

The water had been still, that was until he decided to slam the black orb into the water; the orb plunged down and up came black waves. It spun around, pieces of it branching out to look more akin to sticky kelp pods, but these were as dark as the abyss.

"Don't!" Jager cried out and began to swim toward his brother.

A hum filled the air, that of the Galathea coven, in spite of the soldiers that surrounded the immediate area none had moved. They looked unsure of what to do, the humans were on the land and the one that had plunged beneath the surface was now in the custody of two Mer soldiers.

Oinone looked to her coven, she spoke not a single word but they all seemed to know. This was no longer a fight against the Humans, they had done what they came for and instead, this would turn into a battle against one of their brethren.

As Jager made it to his brother his arms encircled him and he pulled him down into the water, his tail propelled him down as his brother fought against him. "Stop! This isn't you, Kriegen!"

"Yes. it is! They need to be stopped, they need to understand and perhaps if we take *them* out it will send a message to the humans." A burst of water erupted between them and dislodged Jager from him.

Stunned by the blow, he shook his head and glared. "You think that? How about it will cause a war between us and them? How about they will *never* cease seeking out more because it is who they are! Greed runs deep in their veins!"

Kriegen swam up to him and jabbed a finger into his chest. "And here is where it will begin and end. They killed our father, they've slaughtered our kind in the past. When did you become such a lover of the Uplanders? They will never stop, brother, ever. I will take care of you and I will take care of our people." He sneered before continuing. "Even if the cost is great."

Batting away his hand, Jager felt slapped in the face. "I'm not and I never will be. I'm the first one to hold a grudge, but I refuse to make *everyone* pay for what a handful of people were responsible for." In truth, Merfolk were not exempt from cruelties, either.

The sound of water churning brought both of them to a halt, they spun around to witness a wall of waves rushing toward them. Jager attempted to dart away, but was caught in the undertow, he was tossed aside like a pebble.

Kriegen was captured inside of it, it was a net of water intended for him. He grunted as it encased him inside, trapped and unable to break free. He began to chant and his hair came to life around him. The blue faded into his hair and turned as black as Jager's and his voice resounded in the vicinity.

Knocked against a coral reef, Jager felt at his head and saw red bleed into the clear water. He grimaced, shook it off and looked upward, his brother was held in a current that the coven created.

He cursed to himself and pushed himself upward. "To the depths, Kriegen!" he shouted, but no one was around to hear him.

Of all the things to do, turning to the Dark Arts? He shuddered and felt the warm water grow cold, for a moment he thought it was just his imagination, it wasn't.

The water steadily skyrocketed in temperature, as if that wasn't alarming enough it was also darkening, like the orb that had plunged into the sea, the water grew black.

Kriegen wasn't just weaving magic, he was siphoning it from the coven members, he knew this because he could *see* it. The black tentacle-like sinews of water reached out and wrapped around paralyzed members of the coven. Those that were not affected swam away to band together, Oinone was one of them.

A deep laugh resonated in the water as Kriegen began to change before everyone. His hair grew elongated, his fingers stretched out in a horrific display of disfiguration and as he called on the magic of those he drained from his skin blackened.

"Kriegen, stop!" Jager filled with panic as he swam toward him, it was too late, his brother was lost to him and replaced by the maddened creature.

Springs beneath the basin burst and the floor began to crack with an eerie groan. Up came geysers of water that shot from the surface and rained down on the island. The monster swam upward and let one of the geysers shoot him upward. Thick tentacle-like cords of black shot toward the sky and twin waterspouts began to shift over the surface.

Oinone swam up to Jager and grabbed his arm, pulling him away from the black cloud that spread through the water. As it touched the soldiers around them they began to shriek, the blackness speared into them and pulled the bodies into Kriegen. His mass seemed to grow and at the same time it grew thinner, stretched even. Where skin once was now looked to be ink pooling around bone.

"Get back, boy, he'll devour you, too!" she pleaded and pulled him away. "Listen to me, there are survivors, but we have to go down and we have to move fast."

Jager didn't argue as much as he may have wanted to there was nothing that could be done for his brother now. For so long it had been only them and he felt as if he had failed his older brother. "What must we do?"

The pair swam to the surviving members of the coven as well as some of the soldiers.

"We must bind him, there is still hope we can—"

A collective gasp went up as Kriegen sent blackened waves toward the island, they didn't crash on the land but rather rolled beneath the land and like leeches, they clung to the underside.

"Jager! The Tonga Coven was on their way, I sent a conch. Go and see if they have arrived."

"I can stay here, send another— " he began to say.

Oinone's jaw muscles flexed and she sent a chilly glare in his direction. "This is not a time to argue."

As much as Jager wanted to stay here and fight, he knew they needed additional help. Looking down, he saw the crevice that had formed when the geysers shot upward. "Are we to bind him down there?"

Oinone didn't follow his gaze for she was focused on the horror before them. "Yes, it is our only hope at this point."

He nodded grimly as he took up his former teacher's hand. "I will return with aid," he said sadly and offered a squeeze to her hand.

She waved forth the remainder of the coven and

"Dreaux"
by Mirriam Neal

motioned for them to hold hands. "No matter what do not cease singing, do not stop. Close your eyes if you must, but once we begin we cannot stop. If you'd like to leave now it will not be held against you." She waited for a moment but when no one budged she began to pull them into a tight circle.

"May we all sing true, Muir, guide us," she offered and began to sing.

Jager swam away.

The Tonga Coven neighbored Galathea, they were allies and in times of duress, they often lent their aid to coven and Kingdom. Their leader, Lowanna, was ancient, in that she was nearing the end of her days. Still, her magic was strong and in spite of her advanced age, she showed no signs of slowing.

She was also terrifying.

As Jager swam down to the alabaster pillars of their meeting grounds, he saw the stark-white hair wavering in the water. The tell-tale coloring of Lowanna's lower half and the ornamental headpiece she wore told him that she was from the Tonga region.

Her fin was black with stripes of a deep purple which

twined with a soft hue of pink. She had dark skin and a pair of intelligent black eyes stared at him.

"Is it as bad as we think?" she rasped out.

"Yes, darkness has taken one of our own." He purposely left out the fact it was his brother. On the other hand, Lowanna likely knew the truth. She made Oinone's probing gaze look like a shoal's game.

The rest of her coven collected behind her, they were similar in appearance. Dark skinned, but their hair was raven instead of white. Their faces held fluorescent markings on them, some were dots and others stripes. The differentiating markings depicted ranking within the coven, but Jager was clueless as to what dots versus stripes meant.

Besides, now was not the time to ponder over paint.

"May Muir keep him," she brought her hand to her chest and moved it outward, frowning.

He said nothing, he simply mimicked the movement and jerked his head toward the direction they had to swim.

"How long have you known?" she asked him.

Jager would have been taken aback had he not known of her talents, it wasn't known far and wide that Lowanna could read thoughts but Oinone had let it slip a time or two in private.

"Not long enough and too late," he replied shortly.

She nodded her head and propelled herself through

the water with an easy grace. "It's not your fault, boy. He swam in dangerous waters— too extreme in his thoughts. He's not wrong, but the way he thought to handle it is."

A grunt escaped him and he said no more as they swam back to the Island.

They were close enough to the surface that shafts of sunlight should have traveled through the water, yet it didn't. The water was far too murky.

Lowanna immediately swam past Jager and joined up with Oinone, the rest of her coven integrated with Galathea, joining hands and offering greetings.

Jager turned his gaze toward the being that was once his brother.

Whilst he was gone they had successfully trapped him, he writhed around in his bindings, snarling at them.

The Tonga coven chimed in, but Jager could not be party to sealing his brother in a crevice. Memories of fonder times came unbidden and he clenched his jaw so tightly he thought his teeth would snap.

A burst of bubbles came from the deep before the coven lifted up in song. The notes became tangible and formed tendrils that looked much like a streak of lightning. Each strand entangled itself on the mass of writhing black and began to drag him through the water.

Unlike most of the others, he did not close his eyes, he kept them open and watched everything. How the black limbs glued themselves to the bottom of the island, the sound of the eerie groan and hum the ocean took on.

"You don't understand. If it is the island they want it will be the island they get— Forever." Clearly frustrated, he desperately clawed at the water to drag himself away. "They will never stop! Please understand!"

Jager turned away and held his head in his hands, his fingertips bit into his scalp as the groaning of the crevice echoed in the water. His brother began to shriek as the combined covens wove their magic and shoved Kriegen into the deep.

Their magic bound him in place, subduing and trapping him there.

A sob broke free from Jager as he lost the last piece of a family he had, but the sadness fled into anger and when he turned his darkened gaze to the surface he swam toward the soldiers holding Peter.

"You! This is your doing," he hissed his words and scowled. "If it weren't for you this never would have come to be."

A laugh escaped Peter, but Jager wasn't laughing.

His gaze turned the island, the other crew members

that had leaped into the water to avoid burning up with the ship were finding out how big of a mistake this was.

In spite of his anger, Jager's mouth fell open and he watched as a swimming boy clawed at the water and tried to avoid the rip tide that yanked him toward the shore.

The snickering by his side ceased, Peter's mouth parted as he began to cry. The same rip current that had taken the others was now sweeping him and yanking him toward the shoreline. His laughter turned to pleading.

"Help! Stop this!" he cried out.

Jager dipped below the surface and plunged well beneath the island, there was nothing visible to the eye, but he could feel a steady thrum of magic pulsing from it. Kriegen had cursed it? He swam toward it and went to reach out with his magic and promptly felt a throb in his skull.

"What did you do?" He pushed himself backward and felt a hand on his shoulder. He jerked to the side and caught sight of Lowanna and Oinone. "He cursed it?"

"What?" Lowanna cocked her head to the side and eyed the structure. "It should have disappeared when he was sent below."

"Well, it didn't."

"Did you try—" Oinone was cut off.

"I tried reaching out to it and was repelled, but you're more than welcome to try," Jager bit out.

Both of them tried.

And then the three of them tried.

It was of no use, nothing worked. The humans were trapped on their land.

Jager could almost hear his brother's laughter. *They wanted it so badly, now they have it. Now they won't be able to leave.*

"We will have to wait it out, perhaps with time and as his slumber becomes deeper, perhaps it'll weaken and they will be able to leave." Oinone didn't sound as if she believed herself, but who could blame her?

Misery settled inside of him, Jager longed for last week. This week was for the gulls as if things couldn't get any worse.

He should never have thought such a thing.

"Jager of Limnaia?" a voice he didn't know called out.

"Yes, that's me," he said as he spun around.

"You're under arrest for treason."

This had to be some joke. Treason? What in the deep blue had he done that could be considered treason? He had aided in binding his own flesh just a few days prior. He had considered losing himself in one of the towns-folk's brews but would it ease anything long term?

No. Nothing would.

"Are you joking?" He scoffed, but the stern expression on the soldier's face said he was not.

This was absurd, he had done nothing. Since he had done nothing he complied rather than put up a fuss. He knew he'd be hauled off to Selith City and they were all the same— stuffy and couldn't take a joke. They also didn't tolerate anyone swimming out of line.

The palace was a grand place, as it should be. The Uplanders would speak of heaven and what it must look like, Jager imagined it was something akin to the palace. It was a pearl white structure that stood proudly, even at a distance it seemed large, let alone swimming so closely.

As the carriage slowed to a halt, the guards prompted Jager to leave the confines and he grunted as he was shoved between his shoulder blades.

His hands were shackled in front of them and from the middle chain, another section of links lead to a leash the soldier held. Jager had never felt so animalistic than he did now.

"Who is charging me?" he finally asked.

No reply. He shook his head, black hair swirling around him as he had no choice but to follow.

Inside they went, down several halls and inside another corridor and finally inside a room. The King sat in his high back chair and stroked his hairless face, deep in thought.

"The sea whispers secrets, not always ones that hold the truth, but it always talks. It says you knew of your brother's dabblings, is this true?"

How in the depths did he already know that? An accusatory look washed over Jager's face as he spun his head and found none other than Lowanna.

She spread her hands and bowed her head in apology.

"You could have prevented all of this if you had spoken up."

Jager raised his hands which had fisted. "I had just found out. I didn't know previously. By the time I would have reached you and then back again it still would have been too late. None of us knew!"

Oinone would have known better than anyone else and yet she hadn't a clue either. If Jager hadn't stumbled on the hidden compartment of the bookshelf he would have never known either.

"I'll excuse your disrespect this time. Do you have any idea how many lives were lost today?" This was the first time Eidir's voice was raised.

"Forgive me… but Your Majesty, you can't blame me for all—" His voice cut out and he dropped his gaze, he felt frantic inside and felt as if a tidal wave were crushing him. "You do? You blame *me?*"

"If we had known we could have taken him into our custody, lives would have been spared and perhaps the island would not be tainted. Yet, here we are, the bindings on the island haven't loosened after a week, and those wretched Uplanders are still on our land."

Eidir moved from his seat and planted his palms on the table. "As such, you are to be removed from Galathea and banned from using magic. We will not risk another incident like this again." His smooth features rumpled as he eyed down Jager.

"Your Majesty," Lowanna croaked as she moved forward, clearly she didn't expect such a harsh punishment or any punishment judging by the shock on her face.

"Silence! It is either that or execution." His pale eyebrows lifted as he looked to Jager.

"Such options," he muttered.

"Pardon me?" The King drawled, not finding amusement in the cockiness.

"You leave me no choice, Your Majesty. If those are my only options... I have no desire to meet my end yet."

King Eidir nodded his head and moved his gaze behind Jager's shoulder, there was a guard there with shears. "Cut his hair."

Lowanna gasped and clapped her hands together.

"Your Majesty! You cannot. He is a boy, as he said, had he come to you, it still would have been too late!"

It was no use, the King had made up his mind.

Jager struggled, it took three men to pin him down to the floor, the shears did their job and lopped his waist length hair off. Pieces of it floated away in the water.

He couldn't help it, for the umpteenth time this week he wept. His hands went to his head.

A shaming, that was what this was.

Hair to the Merfolk was status, it defined who they were and here he was bald-headed. Everyone would know, if they didn't already.

"Now go and remember no magic, no coven." With that said King Eidir swam from the room and took whatever dignity Jager might have had left.

In the weeks following Jager's sentencing, he discovered that he had become a pariah. His short cropped hair was the talk of the village, and the cities overreacted when they saw him.

They made it a point to move away, to gasp or to pull a child away. It was ridiculous and it stung him. He had never been well received by the townsfolk of Limnaia let alone the city.

The first two weeks he allowed himself to mope and then he could no longer bring himself to live in the house. He sold off the livestock, sold whatever was not dear to him and instead of selling the house he opted to rent it out.

Of course, the bloody thing rotted, because who wanted to live in a house that belonged to *them*?

Which brought him to Megalopolis, a city of business. A place where the prestigious Merfolk dwelled. In contrast to Selith, wealth came first and secondly pedigree. Although even here he received looks of disdain, word traveled fast in this wretched kingdom.

"No matter," he muttered to himself as he swam toward a shop. The first floor was vacant, shelving units within and although it was in need of work, it would do nicely. More importantly, there was a room upstairs.

"So, this is where you'll be?" a familiar voice asked.

"I think so, I think it would be best."

Oinone smiled sadly as she swam up to him, her arms encircled him. "I am so sorry, my boy. My heart aches for you." Her voice cracked as she swept a hand along his bare head.

He cleared his throat and motioned toward the outside of the shop. "I was going to name it Gizmo's, remember that turtle my father had? It refused to come out of its shell unless he was around." A small laugh came from him as he remembered it fondly.

She clasped her hands beneath her chin and smiled. "I do. He was a sweet turtle."

Better than any octopus, he thought sourly and found himself laughing again. "I figured I'd revive his old business, too. Or something similar, I'll figure it out." He rubbed the back of his head and sighed heavily.

"You're a survivor, Jager, I believe you will succeed no matter what."

True enough, he had endured far more than anyone had a right to and perhaps that was why he hadn't caved in on himself. Maybe it was due to the fact that he knew even if he wasn't allowed in the coven or to practice magic that Oinone would not and could not abandon him.

"Oinone," he began, "thank you. Thank you for watching over us." And for not opting to slaughter Kriegen when he likely deserved it. There could still be hope that he would turn to the light again, that once the bindings were loosened and he saw that the Island continued to imprison Uplanders that his mania would cease.

It was a fool's hope, but it was hope nonetheless.

"I will always look out for you, as long as I can." She leaned forward to place a motherly kiss on his cheek and swam away.

Gizmo's would become his livelihood, if he could not

practice magic or do something worthwhile with it, this is what he would become.

He would serve as a reminder to the people of Megalopolis that some secrets could not be buried, no matter how many blind eyes were turned. No matter how many books were destroyed.

The truth would always rise.

About Elle Beaumont

Elle was born and raised in Southeastern, Massachusetts in a little farm town by the harbor. She grew up fascinated with all things whimsical and a strong love for animals.

As she grew so did her passion for reading and writing. Although she prefers devouring all genres she largely enjoys dark fantasy.

She is married to her best friend and has two lively

sprites who inspire madness, love and a sense of humor in her. They also have a menagerie of animals, two dogs, three cats and a horse. In her downtime, Elle enjoys creating candles, crocheting, horseback riding and running.

CONNECT ON SOCIAL MEDIA

facebook.com/ellebeaumontbooks

instagram.com/ellebeaumontbooks

Bloodscales

Amber R. Duell

Winter was late in coming to King Harbor, Massachusetts. Bare branches scraped my bedroom window, but we hadn't bothered to dig our puffy coats out of storage yet. Which would've been great except my high school hadn't used a single snow day and it was nearly Christmas.

"Bri, time for dinner," my mother called.

I rolled off the bed with a sigh. What were the chances it would plummet twenty degrees overnight, and I'd wake up to a foot of snow? I glanced at the craft supplies scattered across my floor. Probably about the same as my finishing the giant project that was due in the morning.

"Tell your father," she added.

"Okay." I padded down the carpeted hallway to my dad's office. The door was cracked, light spilling out, so I poked my head inside. He leaned over his desk, still in his green and khaki park ranger uniform. "Time to eat, Dad."

He glanced at me over his shoulder and smiled. "I'll be there in a minute. I'm on the phone." I took a single step away from the door when his next words froze me in place. "There aren't any mermaids this far north in the Atlantic, especially this late in the year. They must be seeing things."

My ears pricked. Mermaids? In King Harbor? In the fifty-seven years since mermaids became real instead of legend, there had never been a single sighting here. And I would know. I'd spent years combing over the Fish and Wildlife books in my father's office looking for one. Just *one* so I knew it wasn't impossible.

"I don't care how warm the water's been. They've got it wrong." My father paused to let the other person speak. "All right, all right." Another pause. "Yes, I've got it. Down by Peterson's Docks. I'll check it out." Pause. "*Of course* don't put it out on the radio. Do you want poachers to catch wind of it? The last thing we need is a bunch of cutthroats trampling each other over nothing. I'll go see if there's anything there and let you know." He hung up the phone, grumbling.

A mermaid at Peterson's Docks! I held back a burst of giddy laughter. If it was true, this was my chance. All I had to do was get there before my father because he wouldn't let me within a mile of it. Mermaids may have been every bit as majestic as we expected, but some of them were downright vicious.

I raced down the hall. "I'm eating out with Maddie tonight," I shouted toward the kitchen and shoved my feet into my boots.

My mother yelled after me, but it was too late. I sprinted across the lawn to my best friend's house and ran around the back to her bedroom window. "Maddie." I rapped on the glass. "*Maddie.*"

A moment later, Maddie popped into view with a massive messy knot of hair on top of her head. She slid the window open. "Bri? What are you doing out here?"

"Get your shoes and let's go."

"I can't go anywhere. We're leaving for South Carolina in a few hours."

"What? Oh, that's right. Another family fishing trip." I waved a hand through the air. They go fishing all the time, but this was a once in a lifetime opportunity. "You'll be back in time, but we have to hurry."

"I still have to pack and—"

"Madison Campbell, I swear if you don't get your butt out here, I will never forgive you." I leaned closer to the window so I could whisper. "There's a mermaid at Peterson's Docks."

Her face tightened. "What?"

"I just heard my dad on the phone. We have to get there before he does."

"Mermaids? Here?" She narrowed her eyes. "Are you sure?"

I rolled my eyes. "I'll meet you at your truck."

By the time I made it to their driveway, Maddie stood in the open front door, wrapping a knitted scarf around her neck. A stern, imposing figure, hovered behind her, and I wrinkled my nose. Her father was the worst. "Yes, I'm sure," she told him, then hopped outside, pulling her second sneaker on.

"Hi, Mr. Campbell," I yelled. He tightened his jaw and waved. My brows lowered. "What's his problem this time?"

Maddie hurried into her truck and started the engine. "Same old. Probably worried about getting on the road in time so our schedule isn't messed up."

"Well…" I glanced next door at my dad's SUV. "Tick tock on all fronts."

Peterson's Dock was a five minute drive from our houses, eight the way Maddie drove. I was about to jump out on the side of the road and run the rest of the way when she pulled up to the boat launch. I flung myself from the vehicle before it was in park and sprinted into the tall weeds. I motioned for her to join me, but she moved slowly. Too slowly. Just like her driving.

"Come on," I urged. "My dad could be here any second."

Maddie crouched next to me and pursed her lips. "And when he does show up, we're both going to be in a world of trouble."

"Totally worth it *if* we see the mermaid first." I scanned the docks, but nothing moved. Even the water was still. I picked at my lip and crept closer. The rocks along the shore crunched under my weight. It had to be here. *Please, be here.*

"This is stupid," Maddie whispered in my ear. "What if we run into poachers?"

"First." I ticked off a finger. "Why would poachers stake out King Harbor? Second, my father told his coworkers not to call it in so if they're listening in, there's nothing to hear."

"Still, Bri. This is a bad idea."

"How long have you known me?" I stood straight and closed the gap between me and the water's edge.

"Since we were in diapers."

I grinned. "Exactly. So if these last sixteen years have taught you anything, it's that I don't listen to you." Something plunked in the water, and my heart leapt. "There!"

Something red lifted from the low tide and flopped back down helplessly. I rushed forward, and Maddie gripped my elbow.

"It's red," she whispered.

"So?"

"So they're rare and notoriously dangerous. Their—"

Maddie went on about the different ways I could be hurt—killed even—but I barely heard it. Not when what I'd waited so long for was right in front of me, half buried in the dense sand. The young female mermaid's tail was covered in metallic red scales that tapered off halfway up her abdomen. Her skin was the same dark shade, and her hair black as night. She met my eyes for a brief moment, a clear lid flicking over the dark orbs, and released a helpless mewl. I took another step forward, and she tugged helplessly at a fishing net wrapped around her hands, the other end snarled in the wooden dock.

"It's okay," I said quietly. "We're here to help."

My foot splashed in the water, and she let out another heart-wrenching sound.

"Bri, don't. I'm serious," Maddie begged. "Look at it. You'll get yourself killed."

I eyed the long talon-like nails poking from the snarled net and then looked back into the mermaid's eyes. *Help me,* they seemed to say. But they also sparkled with fear, and I knew that scared animals were always the most unpredictable. This was a mermaid though, which meant she was technically half human.

Right?

"Someone has to save her." I took another step into the water, and the cold water seeped in my boot.

"You wanted to see it, and you did." Maddie tugged my arm back toward the truck, but I stood firm. "Your father's coming to take care of it."

"You have a knife in your truck, don't you?"

Maddie kept tugging. "I am *not* letting you use my knife to get yourself killed. Let's go!"

A pair of headlights came around the bend in the road. No one came out to the docks at night. Not even teens looking to party. Because it was regularly patrolled by people like my dad. "Crap."

"Understatement." A spot light scanned the water behind us and Maddie's face dropped. "I thought your dad wasn't calling it in."

"He wasn't."

"Bri, we have to get out of here." She held a hand up against the brightness of the light. "I'm pretty sure those are poachers."

I froze, halfway between running and saving the poor mermaid. "We can't leave it here to get chopped up and sold."

"We most certainly can."

"But we're the only chance she's got." Heat flushed over me, black spots dancing in my vision. If they were poachers…

Maddie hesitated, then pulled a folded knife from her pocket and tossed me the keys. "Go start the truck."

"Why is she bleeding?" I shouted as Maddie peeled out of Peterson's Docks.

Her breath came hard and fast. She peeled off her soaking wet scarf, stained green with mermaid blood. "I hit it with a rock."

I squinted out the back window to where the mermaid was sprawled in the bed of the truck. "You *what*?"

"Oh, I'm sorry. Would you rather it kill me?"

"No, but…" I stared at the poor, unconscious half-girl in the bed of the truck. Green blood trickled down the side of her head. Without eyelids, her black eyes stared up at the night sky as if she were wide awake. "Are you sure you didn't kill *her*?"

"I'm sure." Maddie took a deep breath and let it out slowly. "We'll take it to my family's beach house. It's secluded there."

I rested my chin on the head rest and watched the mermaid jerk back and forth with the movement of the truck. "She's pretty."

"It's a fish."

"What's wrong with you? She's not a fish."

Maddie glared at me from the corner of her eyes. "Bri, really? I wish you hadn't dragged me into this."

"You always say that, but you always have fun when I do."

"You make this sound like some great adventure. Do you realize the trouble we could get into? Mermaids are a protected species, and we're driving around with one in the back of my truck."

I shrugged. "If we're caught, we'll explain about the poachers."

"And what reason are you going to give them about being at the docks in the first place?" She pointed to the glowing time on the dash: 8:48. "I'm not even supposed to be driving after nine."

"Then drive carefully." I grinned at her, but she only tightened her grip on the wheel. "Okay, fine. I'm sorry." I was totally not sorry.

A pair of headlights flicked on from a turn off and pulled out behind us. Maddie fidgeted in her seat. "Can you put your seatbelt on?"

"If it will make you stop whining." I turned around to face forward and clicked my belt in place.

"I'm not whining. Those poachers saw us from the boat. What if they had a team on shore and called to tell them about us? What if that's them?"

My eyes widened. "Okay, Miss Paranoid. This is a main road so there's going to be other cars. Besides, how would you know how poachers work?"

Her face turned bright red. "We have to worry about

them on our fishing trips sometimes."

"Ah." It made sense in a way, though I didn't really see how poachers would be a problem when they were going after fish, but what did I know? The thought of shoving a hook through a worm was enough to make me want to barf. I peeked over my shoulder again. "Do you think she's a princess?"

"Now I know you're messing with me."

"Am not." I crossed my arms. "We don't know everything about them yet. It's totally possible."

"Again, it's a fish. They don't have royal families."

"Did you learn that on your fishing trips too?" I grumbled.

"Why are we friends again?" she scoffed.

I pinched her cheek. "Because our parents are."

"Ha. Ha."

"And because you looove me."

"Unfortunately." Maddie pulled up to a stop sign and hit her blinker. "Which is why I'm taking you home."

"Like Hell you are! You know how much I love mermaids. There's no way you're ditching me now."

"Bri—"

"If you don't turn that blinker off, I'm going to text Grant and tell him everything."

Her jaw dropped, but she quickly snapped it shut. "There's nothing to tell him."

"I'm sure he'd love to hear about the framed picture

you keep of him in your room."

Maddie hesitated. "You wouldn't dare."

"Oh." I raised my eyebrows. "Wouldn't I?"

"You're bluffing."

I unlocked my phone. "Try me."

"If you tell Grant anything, I'll tell Owen you have a crush on him."

A bark of laughter escaped me. "Like he'll believe such an obvious lie."

"*Is* it though? I mean, maybe you only act like you despise him to hide your true feelings."

I reached over and flicked the blinker off. "You'd never do it because it might end up hurting his feelings."

The car behind us honked, and Maddie let out a small groan. "Sometimes I hate you."

The beach house windows were shuttered and dark, making it look as ominous as it always felt. Even as a little kid, I hated coming here for the BBQs and lazy weekends. On one hand, there was the beach two yards away. On the other, seriously negative vibes.

I eased out of the truck and leaned over the back. The mermaid was still unconscious but twitching a bit. Her dry skin looked like tissue paper. The veins throbbed

"Serenity"
by Alicia Gaile

beneath it. The gills at her neck lay flat and still, but her chest rose and fell in shallow rasps.

"They breathe air too," Maddie said, catching my gaze. "It's the drying out you should be worried about."

I glanced toward the sea, trying to calculate how far we would have to carry the mermaid to get her home. Though, if Maddie could drag her to the truck alone at the docks, we should totally be able to carry her to the water together.

"Okay." I wiped my sweaty palms on my jeans. "Let's get her back in the water before she dehydrates."

Maddie glared across the truck at me with something like fear in her eyes. But that wasn't quite it. There was anger there too, and a slice of something I couldn't understand. Finally, she said, "You want to throw it in the water unconscious?"

I shrugged. "She can breathe underwater. Maybe the cold will bring her around."

"Or maybe the tide will wash it up again. Or the current will sweep it further off course."

Valid points. But, as Maddie was the one who knocked her out in the first place, she had to know that once the mermaid woke up, carrying her anywhere would be impossible. "What do you suggest then?"

"The tub." She rolled up her sleeves and pressed her

eyes shut, shaking her head. "I can't believe I'm saying this, but I'll bring up the sea water in a bucket. Like a million times." She glanced at the dark house. "Go open the door. The key's under the flower pot."

I raced up the porch and knocked over every pot until I found the key. By the time I got the door unlocked and opened, Maddie was halfway across the sparse lawn with the mermaid. Her elbows were tucked under the poor girl's armpits, dragging her. A faint trail of green blood caught the moonlight and showed their exact path.

"Wait! You're hurting her." I jumped over the three porch steps and scooped up the base of the mermaid's red tail. The scales were warmer than I expected, and a hard ridge lined the center of each one. I could see myself in the larger ones, the smaller ones reflecting only the night.

"Hit the light," Maddie grunted.

I fumbled inside for the switch with my upper arm until the bulb flicked on overhead. Sweat beaded Maddie's face, and she blew a piece of fallen hair from her eyes. She shuffled backward down the hall, and I followed with strained muscles. Though the mermaid was smaller than the photos I'd seen, she had to weigh at least as much as I did, if not more.

"Careful," I huffed when we finally reached the bathroom. "Don't hit her head again."

Together we shifted sideways and set the mermaid down gently inside the white porcelain tub.

"Oh, my gosh." Maddie leaned back, stretching. "I'm going to feel this tomorrow."

"I'll start bringing in water," I offered.

"No." She pointed to the floor. "You've gotten us into enough trouble. Stay put."

I clicked my tongue. "Don't say I didn't offer."

"That's pretty much the only thing I *can't* accuse you of tonight." She spun on her heel and marched from the room. A moment later, cupboards slammed, and she yelled, "Stay away from it."

When the screen door banged shut, I perched myself on the sink and fixed my gaze on the mermaid. Her hands and arms shook. The skin pulled tight with each small movement and her breath rasped.

"You'll be okay," I whispered.

Maddie stormed back into the room and dumped the water carefully into the tub before stomping back out.

"Don't mind her. I'm pretty sure it hurts her soul to break the rules, but she can be fun when she wants to be."

A soft mewl sounded from the tub, and my pulse spiked. I leaned closer. Was it waking up or was that involuntary?

"What did I say?" Maddie dumped another bucket over the mermaid. "Back away from the tub."

"What's she going to do? Jump halfway across the bathroom with a concussion just to tear me into tiny pieces?"

She grumbled something and left again. And again and again. Twenty seven gallons later, she collapsed on the floor, arms shaking. "That'll have to be enough," she wheezed. "I'm going to go call my dad. They're expecting me home so if I ever want to see the light of day again, I have to tell them something." She shook as she climbed to her feet and fished her phone from her pocket. "You should probably do the same."

I nodded. "My parents think we went to dinner."

"Fine. Let's keep our story straight." She scrolled through her phone. "My truck ran out of gas, and we had to walk to the gas station. That should buy us enough time without making anyone freak out." Maddie glanced up at me, and I nodded. "I'm going outside to avoid an echo." Then she held the phone up to her ear and left.

I unlocked my own phone to send a quick text. *Maddie ran out of gas. Everything's fine, but I'll be home a little later.* "Just you and me again," I said to the mermaid and set the phone down on the sink. When I looked up, the mermaid was staring at me with wide eyes. I gripped the sink to keep from falling.

"Hi." My voice shook. "Are you okay?"

Clear lids flicked over her eyes.

"Can…" I glanced at the door to be sure Maddie wasn't there. "Can you understand me?"

The mermaid didn't move. Then she mewled, and it sounded surprisingly like *yes.* I licked my lips. If she could understand me, I could ask her anything. Maybe she would even answer given the fact that we saved her life. But that was no reason to trust me, really. I could be pretending. *Ugh.*

"You're safe," I said in my most reassuring voice. "My friend and I found you on the beach and saved you from poachers." I eased off the counter. "We wanted to wait until you woke up before putting you back in the ocean so you could swim away."

Her dagger like fingernails crept over the side of the tub. Each one clinked against the porcelain. "H…" She pulled herself up a little more. "Ho… Home."

Or at least, I think that's what she said. It was a bit like a whale call and a cat's meow smushed together.

"Yes, home." I smiled. "When my friend gets back, we'll carry you to the water."

At least, I hoped so. Would Maddie get close to her now that she was awake? It would take two seconds for her to kill her with those fingers. The tub was Maddie's idea—maybe she had a better one for getting her out.

"My dad's on his way." Maddie stepped back into the bathroom, rubbing a hand over her hair. "We're busted. Your mom talked to mine, and they knew we weren't at dinner. But on the plus side, he'll know what to—" She leapt back into the hall. "When did it wake up?"

"Just now." I waved a hand impatiently. "You told your parents *the truth*? You could've made up a hundred lies."

"I could have, but we're in way over our heads here," she snapped.

"She's awake now. We can put her back and be home in no time." Now, on top of being in trouble for lying and breaking curfew, there was smuggling a protected species. I was going to be grounded until I hit thirty.

"Yeah." She snorted. "Like I'm touching it now."

"She's not going to hurt you." I shifted to face the mermaid. "Are you?" She snatched her sharp fingers back into the tub. "See? She just wants to go home."

"Right." She rolled her eyes. "We're waiting for my dad to get here."

"That's stupid. We can manage."

"Because it told you so? And it's so trustworthy?" she growled. "Nope. I'll wait on the porch."

I glanced between her and the mermaid. "I can't carry you alone," I told her. "You're too heavy."

She splashed water up her chest and sunk into the tub so all I could see of her was the top of her head and eyes.

"I'll talk to her. Hold on."

I slipped out of the bathroom and tip-toed through the quiet beach house. It was half lived-in, giving it an empty, lifeless feeling. They kept the house next to mine so Maddie could go to the better schools, but still, it felt odd to own two homes so close to each other.

Outside, two voices exchanged a hushed conversation. But it couldn't be Maddie's dad already. She just talked to him, and it's at least a fifteen minute drive.

"She doesn't know anything, Dad," Maddie whispered. "Leave her alone."

"You put our entire family at risk," her father growled.

"What did you want me to do?"

"You should've left it on the beach."

"I saw the SUV coming, but there were poachers in a boat, Dad. They must've had a tracker on it or something."

"Just get Bri out of here."

The screen door creaked when I pushed it open. "Hey, Mr. Campbell."

"Bri," he said roughly. "Get in Maddie's truck. She'll take you home, and we'll deal with you two later."

"I can help," I offered sheepishly.

"I think you've done enough." He pointed to the truck, and I trudged toward it. "Maddie, show me where this thing is before you go."

"I'll be right back, Bri." She clenched her fists and disappeared into the house, her father on her heels.

I'd come this far, and I wouldn't even get to see her swim away? It didn't seem fair, but I went to the truck anyway. The only thing that could possibly make things worse was my parents hearing I didn't listen to Mr. Campbell. *You just wanted to* see *one,* I reminded myself. Everything else that happened was risky and stupid, like

Maddie said. But she didn't seem very worried about Mr. Campbell being attacked in the process of releasing the mermaid. There wouldn't even be anyone here to call for help if things went wrong.

Call.

Crap. My phone was still on the sink.

I sprinted back into the house and down the hall to the bathroom. The mermaid squealed and the photos on the wall shook. My stomach dropped, the room spinning. Mr. Campbell stood over the tub with a large knife. Maddie had the mermaid in a choke hold with thick gloves going all the way to her elbow.

The mermaid's second squeal cut off as quickly as the glint on the blade. Maddie released the mermaid and peeled the gloves off.

"I can't believe you found a Bloodscale," Mr. Campbell said. We're going to be set for a long time. It almost makes all the trouble you caused tonight worth it."

Maddie nodded, not looking at the spray of green blood on the wall. But it was all I could see. That and the awkward twist of the tail jetting over the edge of the tub.

"I'll break it down and prep everything for sale. Get Bri home—make sure she thinks I released it—and tell your mother to have the camera ready. These scales are going to go fast."

"Does this mean the fishing trip is off?" Maddie asked.

Mr. Campbell shrugged. "I suppose we could still go,

but a Sunscale isn't really worth tracking after this. Maybe we'll take a vacation instead."

Maddie nodded and flopped the gloves onto the sink. Right next to my phone. She paused and picked it up as if it might explode. Then her eyes snapped to mine and the color drained from her face. She moved toward me as if she wanted me to run. "I'll see you at home," she blurted.

Then her fingers dug into my arm as she dragged me away. I let her. I couldn't do anything else. My body had forgotten how to move on its own, my tongue too heavy to form words, even if my brain remembered what those were.

"You were supposed to wait in the truck," Maddie hissed.

Outside.

We were outside.

The cold night air slapped my face.

"Bri!"

No. It was Maddie slapping me.

"What…" I gasped for air. "What just happened?"

"I told you we might run into poachers."

I swallowed the lump in my throat. "You didn't say you *were* poachers."

"It's not what it looks like," Maddie said. "And if anyone finds out you know, they'll kill you."

"Which is it?" My voice rose until it was nothing more

than a squeak. “If you’re not poachers, what will they kill me for, Madison?”

“You’re still here?” Mr. Campbell called from the porch. I spun to face him, and the moment I did, the moment he saw my face, he knew. I had seen. I knew his secret. I knew the mermaid was dead inside their bathroom. “Oh,” was all he said.

“Dad, no,” Maddie begged. “She won’t say anything. Will you, Bri? You’re not going to say anything.”

“I…” Would I? They were murderers. If I didn’t say anything, I would be just as bad. But I also had to get out of here… “No. I won’t. I swear.”

Her father shook his head. “We can’t take that chance, Maddie.”

“It’s not a chance. It’s *Bri.* We’ve known her forever. She’s like a sister to me.”

“She may feel like your sister, but she’s not.” He was in the driveway, gripping my arm before I knew what was happening. “Nothing personal, Bri, but this is a family business.”

In less than a second, Mr. Campbell had me against the side of the truck, his hands around my throat. I clawed at his arms, kicked at his legs. I opened my mouth to beg him, beg Maddie, but I couldn’t. Maddie’s cries for him to stop lowered into a buzz. My vision tunneled, my lids heavy.

Then there was nothing but black.

My eyes cracked.

The bathroom.

I was in the bathroom surrounded by green blood. Dried. Darker. Nearly triple the amount. I rolled my head against the tile and pain shot through my neck. Mr. Campbell leaned over the tub, pliers in hand and a bucket of red scales beside him.

Move, I urged myself. He was preoccupied. I just had to roll into the hall and make a break for it.

But Maddie's father seemed to sense the very thought. He twisted around and winced. "Forgive me, Bri. I didn't want for this to happen." He set the pliers down and wiped his hands on a green-stained butcher's apron. "I shouldn't have attacked you like that."

"Please," I rasped. *Green. So much green.* His hands were spotted with dried patches. I pushed myself up onto my elbows. "You don't have to do this."

"I know. Maddie stopped me before it was too late."

My arms relaxed and slid out from beneath me. I wasn't going to die. Of course not. This was Mr. Campbell. He might've been overbearing and a bit of a jerk, but he wasn't going to kill me. My parents were his best friends, his daughter mine. Maddie called the mermaid a fish—I supposed they had to think that way in their line of work—but I was a human. It wasn't the same. He wasn't a murderer.

"Maddie and I talked while you were asleep," he continued. "You may not be blood, but you've been a part of our family since you were born. So, if you're willing, this is your chance to join us."

My breath caught. He couldn't mean… "Join you?"

"With Maddie's brother off at college, we're down a set of hands."

Me? Hunt and kill mermaids? After talking to it? After knowing they understood? I couldn't do that. Could I? No. Absolutely not. Unless I pretended so I could save the mermaids they found. I glanced at the tub and swallowed against the nausea. If I couldn't save her tonight, how could I save any in the future?

"Mr. Campbell, I… I can't even kill a spider."

"I was afraid of that." He leaned back on his heels. "But Maddie convinced me to make the offer."

"Wait." I scrambled back until I hit the wall. "Wait!"

But the pressure was back on my neck. I flailed. I couldn't go out like this. My hand brushed the pliers. I gripped them and swung. The metal thudded helplessly against his side. My vision came and went a second time. Heat swept up my back.

Maddie stepped into the doorway, eyes puffy with tears. *I'm sorry,* she mouthed.

About Amber R. Duell

Amber R. Duell was born and raised in a small town in Central New York. While it will always be home, she's constantly moving with her husband and two sons as a military wife. Before becoming published, she had a wide range of occupations including banking, bartending (though she's never tried alcohol), and phlebotomy (though she faints with needles). She also volunteered as a re-enactor at the local Revolutionary War fort and worked near shelter cats which led to her previous crazy cat lady status.

CONNECT ON SOCIAL MEDIA

facebook.com/amberrduellauthor

instagram.com/amberrduell

twitter.com/amberr_duell

ALSO BY AMBER R. DUELL

Fragile Chaos

The Last Goodbye: A Fragile Chaos Novella

Dream Keeper (Feb 2019)

Tails, You Lose

E.J. Hagadorn

The day I took my last breath of air, I couldn't tell what made me feel worse: the lurching of my stomach as I rattled down the dirt road, or the house I was about to invade.

Owning an antique shop had plenty of perks, especially for someone who loved history, but the best was having a lucrative side hustle working for the local probate attorney. Whenever someone died, and something valuable needed to be appraised, he always hired me. I was starting to think he just wanted an excuse to see me.

The road sloped and curved through the brown hills. I rounded a dry cove and finally saw the house up ahead. It was a rickety pile of wood, resting off a low cliff and leaning on seaweed-covered pylons, with the surf rushing and crashing against the rocks underneath. I felt nervous. Based on what little I knew about this man, I wasn't expecting this to be a pleasant trip.

His name was Sebastian Wooding. I suppose every town has someone like him; the sort who's been through the ringer once or twice and come out a little messed up. He had a crazed look in his eyes, and you could always tell he was coming by the smell. He seldom spoke to anyone, and when he did, he muttered in whisky breaths.

He was a fisherman by trade, but not a very good one. He'd become a kind of laughing stock among the other bait-slinging salts in town.

Then one day Sebastian disappeared. For a whole day and night, his spot in the marina remained empty. It didn't take long for people to start hoping he'd sailed away for good. I'm a little ashamed to say I was one of those people. After a lifetime spent in foster care, I should have known better.

On the following morning, his boat washed ashore completely empty. No fish, and no Sebastian. Only a thick spot of blood on the railing. For days, theories were tossed every which way about how he died, and where the body was. For a town that didn't seem to like Sebastian, they sure seemed incredibly concerned about his death.

I wasn't surprised to learn he had no heirs. As a result, everything of Sebastian's – his boat, his house and everything in it – was now going to an estate sale.

And that's how I wound up at his front door.

As I observed the house, with the starfish and

"Blue Mer"
by Madeline Elwood

seashells ornamenting the windowsills and the anchor-shaped knocker, I thought it looked kind of cool. It had a real nautical atmosphere to it. I opened the door with the key Mr. Tiler had given me.

I gazed around the house for a few moments, awestruck and stupidly bewildered. Then I reached into my bag and pulled out a BINGO card. Each square had something written on it: *Chinese Vase, Celtic Sword, Clown Doll, BDSM Dungeon,* and all sorts of other things. I took it with me on every assignment. Whenever I found one of those things in a dead person's house, I would cross it off the card. It was creepy, but after spending my childhood moving from one family to another, I'd learned to take my jollies where I could get them.

The last square was *Taxidermy.*

The inside of Sebastian's house was overflowing with stuffed and mounted sea creatures. Stingrays, octopi and fish of all sizes swam along the walls. Sea urchins and crabs sat on tables and shelves. A pair of shark jaws hung wide over an ancient TV set, while a swordfish curved up toward the ceiling. There must have been nearly two-dozen different species in that house, and their glass eyes gazed at me wherever I went.

What I liked most was a painting hanging beneath the swordfish. The subject was a beautiful mermaid sitting on a rock, with a long blue tail and dark hair that was whipped in her eyes by a storm. The clouds were grey, and out at sea, a ship was fighting the wind. Seeing it made me feel a mixture of bravery, sadness, and trepidation. I looked at the signature in the bottom right-hand corner and my jaw dropped.

"Who the heck are you, Sebastian?"

The rich decorations kept me riveted for quite a while, but eventually I remembered I had a job to do. Mr. Tiler had said he was going to come and see the house later, and I wanted to finish before he arrived. I clicked a pen and got started.

The first few rooms were surprisingly clean for an old bachelor's place. The furniture looked like it had been sitting in the same position for years. A small bookshelf was stuffed with books of mythology and the occult, a detail I didn't think about too much at the time.

I peeked in the bathroom and saw that the toilet was nothing but a hollowed-out wooden chair mounted over a hole in the floor, with the waves washing around underneath. Gross.

After that, all that was left was the workshop.

I opened the door, and was knocked back by the most horrible rotten fish smell I'd ever encountered in my life.

On the table before me was an enormous pile of fish guts. Scales and stomachs and thick meaty loins lay heaped up, oozing and dripping onto the floor.

Flies scattered as I stepped inside. The room stretched the entire length of the house, like a porch with grimy glass windows.

Under the window was a worktable as long as the room itself. It was covered with fishing lines, buoys, lobster traps and coils of rope. Hanging from the ceiling were tons of creepy-looking tools. This must have been where Sebastian did his taxidermy.

Pulling on a pair of rubber gloves from the kitchen, I gradually cleared away the fish guts, dropping them handful by handful down the toilet hole.

Then I found what must have been Sebastian's latest project.

On the worktable, hidden under a wrapped-up net, was a mermaid's tail. Just calling it that sounded weird, but it was the only way I could describe it. Part of me wanted to catalogue the thing. The rest of me was a little afraid. After all, why would a 60-something-year-old man use taxidermy to make himself a fake mermaid tail? I suddenly felt like I was walking around in a foggy dream.

I touched it. It felt real.

It felt wet.

Moreover, the entire tail, from scales to fin, was one long, seamless stretch of skin, as if it had come from one big fish.

I examined the tail for a long time, until a sharp

knock at the door brought me to my senses. It was Mr. Tiler. I hid the tail under the net once again and went to let him in.

That night I couldn't sleep. I don't think anyone could.

It was funny that a guy called Sebastian would make a mermaid tail. Ha-ha funny, and weird funny. I'd heard of people who did this sort of thing in other places. Performers at aquariums and Hawaiian hotels wore tails made of spandex and silicone and put on shows for kids. They called it 'mermaiding.' A strange hobby for a man like Sebastian, but who was I to be surprised?

As I lay awake in bed, and the clock struck midnight, I laughed a little. I could still remember wishing to be a mermaid every birthday as a girl. What were the odds that someone like that would find a fake mermaid tail in such a random place?

I lifted the covers and checked. Two legs, same as always.

Then I got an idea, and I didn't like it one bit. It was crazy, creepy, and probably illegal.

I got out of bed, got into the car in my pajamas, and drove out of town.

The house was dark, as dark as it can get. I flicked a switch, but nothing happened. I'd forgotten the power was disconnected.

I groped my way through the rooms. I could sense all the taxidermy eyes watching me in the darkness.

Then I got to the workshop. The waning moonlight barely lit up the room. The tail was still there, which surprised me for some reason.

I don't know how long I stood in front of it. I don't even know what I thought about. I just stood there in my pj's and my coat, and I looked at it.

Had this leathery-feeling skin all come from one creature? I tried to imagine what kind of fish could be this big, but all I could think of was the mermaid portrait in the living room. I looked around at all the fishing hooks and taxidermy saws hanging around me, and I shuddered at the thought.

I shook my head and took off my coat. If I was going to do this, I had to get it over with.

I removed my pajama bottoms and picked up the tail without another thought. I sat on the floor and slipped my legs inside.

It was a tight squeeze, but it fit perfectly.

And there I sat, looking at the tail in the dark.

I giggled a little. All this trouble so I could try on what was basically a costume piece. I felt a little stupid, but in a good way. It would've made a great story, not that I was planning on telling anyone.

With my night's work accomplished, I tugged on the fins.

Nothing happened.

I felt around my waist for the seam.

I couldn't find it.

My heart started to race. No way was I going to get stuck in a mermaid costume in a dead guy's house.

I messed around in the dim light, looking for a zipper or something, but there was nothing there. I ran my hands up and down the scales trying to push the thing off me, but it didn't work. It was so tight on my legs the friction actually hurt.

With panic flooding my mind, I reached up onto the table and grabbed the first knife handle I found.

I held the knife shakily and sliced the tail.

I screamed and fell over.

I dragged myself into the living room. Then something changed. A tingling feeling of pain, like a thousand flu shots, was working its way out of my tail and into my body. My eyes filled up with tears. My ribs ached. My hands clenched.

When it was all over I opened my eyes. I could see everything in the pitch-black room.

I felt my sides under my pajama top. I had gills!

And I was suffocating.

I thrashed around. The tail flew from side to side, knocking over lamps and chairs and occult books.

Overhead I could see the room swaying, and it looked like the taxidermy fish and crabs had come to life. They bobbed and bowed, mocking me as they swam through the air.

My body fell limp. All the air was gone. I lay on my side, and I saw light coming out of the floor. It was the bathroom.

My hands moved. My gills flapped, frayed and dry and desperate. One hand over the other, I pulled myself up to the toilet hole, slid down, and splashed into the glorious life-giving firmament of the ocean.

For the last thirty years, neither I, nor my sisters, nor the bones of Sebastian Wooding, have ever breached the surface.

About E.J. Hagadorn

E.J. Hagadorn is the author of numerous works of macabre fiction and poetry. When not writing, he is often found going on road trips, lurking in graveyards, or sleeping at his desk.

His work may be found at www.ejhagadorn.com, and he blogs about dead authors at www.authorgraves.com.

CONNECT ON SOCIAL MEDIA

instagram.com/oscar_and_edgar

SKY ABOVE

THE COUNTRY OF STENFISK OVERLOOKED THE KLENOD SEA and the palace stood proudly on a cliffside. The waves hurled themselves at the stony sides savagely, as if wanting to claim the land for itself. It would serve the crown right if it did, but that was another matter entirely.

Below the cliffside a rasping noise spewed forth, accompanied by a sputtering as a tan face emerged from the white caps. A ragged intake of breath melded in with the sound of the crashing waves and laughter came forth. A pair of black eyes opened and slammed shut, Zinnia felt the sun's rays on her face and smiled in triumph.

"Oh, holy depths," she murmured and pressed her fingers against her face. There was no gentle breeze, it was a turbulent day and it hurled the sea violently and disrupted her smoothed back hair.

She blinked away the bright spots in her vision and

stared up at the structure above once she moved her hands. Curiosity had gotten the better of the young Mermaid and she opted to break one of the rules: Never surface.

Zinnia, daughter of Kohl, felt peace and she reveled in it. Tomorrow would be life-changing, in one way or another.

A violent whoosh of water protruded from the surface and a rattling breath was drawn in, it surprised Zinnia and made her turn around and she stared owlishly at the individual who rubbed their eyes viciously.

"Dru?" she asked incredulously.

"The light is going to burn my eyes from their sockets!" he complained and slammed his eyes shut.

Zinnia laughed softly, Dru had been a friend for greater than a decade. Their friendship defied many odds, he was a Lord and heir to a great fortune in Megalopolis, while she was only an apothecary's daughter and lived in Limnaia. The latter of which was a farming village that produced kelp and Hippocampus for the rest of the Kingdom. Such things shouldn't matter, but they did, Selith held on to the old ways and traditions with a vice grip.

"Your eyes are not going to be burned, look, open them slowly and raise a hand up to your forehead." She took one of Dru's hands and lifted it to his forehead to shield the sun and when he opened his crystalline eyes she laughed again. "See? No scorched eyeballs," she said and lifted an eyebrow.

"You shouldn't be up here," Dru's voice trailed as he glanced up at the palace, a small noise leaving him.

"Yes, well, to be fair you shouldn't be my friend and yet you are." She swam next to him and tread the water. Dru's skin was porcelain and Zinnia's was sandalwood. She had thick black hair, with dark intelligent eyes. Dru had the same black hair, but his eyes were an icy blue which set against pale skin lent him an eerie look.

"Semantics, I don't really give a gill what anyone thinks," he offered and grinned at her. "I'm all for adventures, but this one… I say we should get back to the depths." Dru looked uneasy, his pale face looked slightly green.

"Are you nervous?" Zinnia inquired. "No one will see us here," she began to say but heard a yell, it was a ship pulling up to the docks. She took Dru's hand and pulled him into the depths once again. "Better?"

"I suppose you count them as nothing, then?" Dru offered, his full lips quivering as he attempted to keep a stern expression.

"Hm, yes, they didn't see us and therefore they are *nothing*," Zinnia retorted. She wasn't so curious as to explore the human world, she simply wanted to see it. "You're not at least a little excited about having gulped down your first mouthful of fresh air?" Zinnia's eyes darted to her friend as she swam a distance away from him.

Dru's eyes rolled as he followed suit. "Okay, maybe a little. Once I realized you - we - were not in imminent danger." His tail flicked downward and propelled him past Zinnia. Dru's tail was a rich, dark blue with accents of black, it lent him a look of a predator.

Zinnia's eyes widened as he floated in front, the look quickly faded as she used her tail to spin around him. Unlike her friend's tail, she had several frills that floated in the current, it had an assortment of pink, orange, and red.

"I'll race you back," Dru flicked a piece of hair away from his face.

"Okay, challenge accepted." Zinnia grinned and darted off through the water.

Once they had made it back to the city of Megalopolis, both were huffing and puffing, their mouths split into wide grins as they laughed. Of course, Dru had won, he was a great deal taller than Zinnia and he was athletic to boot. Zinnia was not, she wasn't afraid to admit that. She was much better at books than sports.

"Well done, Dru," she said, panting softly.

They each received condescending looks from the nearby Mer. To say the city was stuffy would be an understatement, not only that but Zinnia was clearly not of wealth and was seen as something akin to an urchin.

"Nice try." A cackle slipped from him once he caught his breath. Dru's gaze slowly lost the mischievous glint as they locked onto a carriage in the distance.

Zinnia nudged his arm with an elbow and kept her voice low. "Are you okay?" Dru?" she found herself whispering.

"That's… a royal carriage," he stated and eyed the crowd that quickly gathered around. A soft murmur began to rise up around the area.

The notion of a royal in the heart of the city wasn't strange, it was, however, strange that one would be present without a scheduled tour. For the most part, the Royals stuck to scheduling events and reasons to mingle with the Merfolk outside of the capital of Selith, yet here they were or at least one was.

There were guards that flocked around the carriage which blocked the view of who it could have been, but Dru was having none of this and so he took up Zinnia's hand and led her toward the crowd. Everyone murmured their thoughts, but nothing was clear as to what was happening.

"Get back," a guard groused loudly, a sword was held across his person. A scowl on the guard's face said that he had every intention of using it should someone disobey. "I said get back!" he shouted again.

A frisson ran along Zinnia's spine as she watched with wide eyes and unbeknownst to her she had grabbed a hold of Dru's arm, her fingers pressed into his skin as the next events unfolded.

White blond hair swirled in the current around a tall Merman, Zinnia felt the air seize in her lungs as she spotted Prince Loch angrily swimming from a shop. Behind him was an equally ornery individual. His hair was cut so short he was nearly bald, which was strange because their people prided themselves in their appearances. Their hair symbolized a lot and to be without any? It was almost a shameful thing.

"You may not enter my shop without reason! I have done nothing!" The man cried out, the expression on his face was not one of a humble servant of the crown. He could have been handsome if it weren't for the scowl that warped his features.

Prince Loch whipped his head around and charged in front of the man, who was only a hair shorter. "I am your Prince, the heir to the throne, is that not enough reasoning for you? I need no other reason, Jager," he hissed.

The name tickled something at the back of Zinnia's head, a story from long ago, but it was difficult to grasp

"Zinnia"
by Madeline Elwood

and felt like it was tangled in new memories. Why did that name sound so familiar?

"You may be *the* Prince, *Your Highness*, but you are not yet King," Jager responded smoothly and his voice was surprisingly steady. He did not balk when the Prince loomed closer, his hands were relaxed to the sides, however, his jaw flexed in frustration.

"Watch yourself, *Witch*, everyone may have forgotten what happened, but the Royal family has not," Prince Loch spat his words at the other. "He is clear, for now," he said to the nearby guards and motioned with a hand for them to follow.

Jager stood in the doorway of the shop, *Gizmo's*, as he glowered at the nearby crowd. "Move along, this isn't a sideshow," he ordered and turned his back on the crowd to escape into the shop.

"What was that about?" Zinnia realized she had been clutching tightly onto Dru's arm, hard enough to leave marks and released it at once.

"I don't know, Jager never bothers anyone," Dru muttered, his shoulders slumping as he looked down at his arm. "Did you have to squeeze me so hard?" He rubbed it and made a face.

"Dru, he is a witch, what do you suppose Prince Loch meant by that?" Zinnia asked quietly as the knowledge settled into her mind and clashed with the stories.

"I don't know," he whispered softly.

Zinnia did not want to settle for that, she snapped her fingers and her eyes widened. "I salvaged one of the history volumes that was set to be destroyed, maybe it will enlighten us." She looked hopeful as Dru began to tug on her hand.

"Let's get you back home, I don't want your mother chiding me, she's worse than what my nursemaid was." Dru shuddered, only half joking. "Also, leave it to you to pull a volume from ruin."

"Don't forget, we have to study for the Trial, too." Zinnia worried on her lower lip, she didn't want to think about the that, not after what she had just seen and yet there was no way around it.

Selith's finest attended the Academy and if a Mer were fortunate enough they could shell out enough currency to afford the curriculum for their child. Zinnia was not wealthy but her father had constructed a comfortable enough cushion for her to attend a school that was otherwise out of her reach.

As it happened, Selith was hosting a Trial this year, which occurred once every twelfth year. The event selected not one but two of the Academy's finest students who would be dubbed superior students and should they want for it, to join a coven. The subject over the years had become a touchy one and magic seemed to be dying out in their kind, but some clung to it like a lifeline because it was all they had attached to their name.

Dru slapped a hand against his face harder than he anticipated and cursed to himself. "You had to remind me."

"Someone has to keep you on track," she giggled as she swam away from him and in spite of the earlier tension she allowed giddiness to run through her. She wove in and out of the crowd in the city, darted away from a cart that pulled out in front of her and pushed further away from Dru. He'd catch up eventually, but for the moment Zinnia was in the lead, winning and carefree.

As predicted, Dru caught up in no time. His face split into a grin as he pointed at her. "You're getting better at slipping away, sneaky," he said and pulled away. "Zin, I'm going to ask around as to what happened at Jager's before we showed up. Something doesn't feel right." Dru pressed his lips together in a grim line.

"I know, I don't like it either. Before I study I'm going to pull out my old volumes and see what I can find." It was one of the only volumes that contained the story of the Dark, all the others had been ripped from their owners and destroyed. There had been a time where people feared that the darkness would spread throughout the city and that it would infect the people, that magic would taint everyone.

"Okay, the sooner I get you home the sooner I can get back here to figure out what is going on, or at least a little of it." Dru moved toward an awaiting carriage and shelled out currency to the awaiting driver and helped Zinnia in. "To Limnaia," he said to the driver and settled in beside Zinnia as they left.

SEA BELOW

Luck had been on Dru's side when he arrived in front of the humble home and Aminta, Zinnia's mother, was still at work, which meant she could easily slip inside the house and make it appear as if she had been there for hours. So, she did just that and pulled out the crumbling volume that covered Kriegen. Zinnia's fingers paused over the text, this had happened several hundred years ago and while it was no secret that the Mer lived a lengthy life, Jager certainly didn't look as if he were pushing five hundred years, yet he was.

She opened the book and felt her heart seize, it was silly to feel this way but she felt as if someone or something was watching her. She felt as though what she was doing was somehow wrong. Of course, that was entirely silly of her but it didn't help matters.

"Kriegen, where are you?" she muttered to herself as she flicked through the pages and halted at the text that glared at her. *The Dark Time* glared up at her and she devoured the text that came next.

The brothers Kriegen and Jager had been valued members of society, they were seen as protectors of the realm because when it was needed it was they who pulled the surrounding covens together. They were powerful individually, but when they combined their magic they were nearly unstoppable.

It is known that the Uplanders or rather humans *cannot be trusted. They speak words they do not mean and make promises they cannot keep. Our beloved King Eidir proclaimed if they should ever think to trespass on our waters, if they should take what is not theirs then they would pay dearly.*

So when that time came to pass, when the humans dared to claim a piece of our waters, our land, the brothers rallied against them.

Kriegen was stronger than Jager and he knew it. He fought against the humans, much to his brother's dismay and he called upon every magical cell in his being to ensure that they would not take that which didn't belong to them.

Amidst the battle, blackness swirled in the sea, tainting the blue with an inky substance. It consumed everyone, but it was Kriegen's shrill scream that filled the current and air alike.

Jager hadn't been in the vicinity, he had been spared and when he surfaced to spy on the land which had been secured, he saw the carnage there and in the sea around him.

While he mourned for his brother that had been lost, the kingdom painted him as a pariah and the crown blamed him for the Dark and the death that surrounded. His heroics had been forgotten, the good he had done soon erased.

He became an outcast.

Zinnia blinked her eyes and she wondered if there was more to it. The text was so vague, she grumbled and shut the volume carefully. There had to be more to it than just that. Maybe Dru could uncover more of the story.

She was so lost in her thoughts she didn't hear her mother swim into the room and when she touched her shoulder Zinnia leaped from her chair. "Mother!" she cried out.

Aminta's almond-shaped eyes narrowed and she cocked her head to the side. "Are you alright, Zinnia? I called out to you when I came in," she said with a laugh, but concern and confusion warred with the laughter.

"Yes, you just scared me. I was reading and you know how I get with books." She laughed at herself and how she became so submersed into a book.

"Are you hungry? You need to eat, tomorrow is a big day for you." She turned her dark eyes on her daughter and tucked a loose strand of hair behind her ear.

"Oh, don't remind me. Dru and I are going to be ill," she covered her mouth to dramatize it which made her mother laugh.

There was something in her mother's gaze that Zinnia could not discern as she swam away, and Zinnia let it go. Studying wouldn't go over so well if she didn't have food to fuel her. Food was a temporary distraction from the current stresses in her life and the budding feeling that something more was going on.

It could wait until tomorrow until she could corner Dru and discuss their findings. For now, it was time to eat and then back to studying.

Morning came quickly, too quickly. A frown crept across the tanned face of Zinnia, lost in a world of dreams and whirls of color, she felt turbulence in her dream. Blackened faces, hollowed out eyes and screams surrounded her. Panic gripped her, she saw a looming figure and when it turned its soulless eyes on her she let out a scream until the deep sound of the gong in town entered her mind. She sat upright and she covered her face with her hands, almond-shaped eyes widened in a moment of panic.

She was okay, it was just a dream, but the panic felt so real. Zinnia relaxed some until realization dawned on her.

“No! Oh no. I’m going to be late,” she whispered to herself as she flung her blanket off. The gong sounded again, and again until the total clangs amounted to seven. Seven o’clock in the morning and she was going to be late to the academy. Today of all days, too! The day of the

Trial! She dragged a coral comb through her hair quickly and in the process pulled thick wads of black hair out and grimaced. There would be no time to fuss over her appearance, not that she generally did anyway.

Zinnia was top of the class and it was by no fluke, she had worked for it, had studied harder than any Mer that went to Selith's finest school. She was not privileged like so many others. Some of the elite referred to her as a bottom feeder, because she was not born in Megalopolis. No, she was born in Limnaia, where the backbone of society was born and bred. The farmers, the small business owners. Zinnia was proud of who she was and where she had come from, but to say it didn't sting as much as a jelly would be nothing short of a lie.

"To the depths," she muttered as she swam through the small hallway in her family home. She rounded a corner, the sound of her bangles clanging reverberated in the current. She may not have had bejeweled shells to adorn her hair, but Zinnia had her bangles and the sheer gown she wore had been spun and dyed herself from the local kelp groves.

"Zinnia, my love!" Came the exasperated exclamation. Aminta shook her head as she swam toward her daughter, took stock of her appearance and fretted over it. She knew that today was important for her daughter, it meant more than just winning a plaque, it meant she deserved to be amongst those snobby elites. She didn't need to win to prove that, but such were a mother's thoughts.

"I know, I know, I'm going to be late," Zinnia peered over her mother's shoulder and toward the exit of their home.

"It is not that, my love. You look so much like him, you know? Your father… he would be… You are beautiful and smart, take a moment and you will pass today's test. I'll be there in the stands." Aminta's almond-shaped eyes formed slits as she smiled broadly, she bit her bottom lip and refrained from finishing her prior statement.

Zinnia may have felt exasperated that she was being delayed but she basked in her mother's affection. The mention of her father caused her heart to twist because they both missed him. It had been two years since he passed away and not a day went by they didn't feel his absence. She would win this for him or at least she would try. She leaned forward to press her cheek against her mother's. "I'll look for you," she whispered and pulled back before she began to swim out the door.

Thank the gods there were no more obstacles in her path, Zinnia arrived fashionably late. Most of the other

Mer were seated already, but she wasn't the only one to file in late and so she was hardly noticed.

Dru was seated in the middle of the auditorium and she noticed a seat had been saved. So much for discussing findings before the Trial began. Zinnia stared ahead at the podium where her mistress was seated and worried on her lower lip.

"You're lucky she didn't notice you," Dru murmured.

Zinnia's eyes flicked over to her friend and she pressed her lips together to hold in a laugh. "I know, thanks for saving me a spot," she whispered. Everything felt surreal, a decade ago she had been new to the academy and certainly known as an outcast, but Dru, who came from a noble family had turned his back on Society's thoughts and glued himself to Zinnia as if he were a barnacle in a prior life. Back then she had figured it was simply a pity friendship, but as the years passed it was clear that he had no intentions of parting from her. Zinnia's eyes softened as she looked at him and when silence settled over the crowd, her eyes moved to Mistress Oinone.

There would be time to discuss their findings later, but for now, the rest of her life was at stake.

Mistress Oinone perched on a stone seat, her bright red hair coiled on top of her head, which lent her a rather severe look, but it was not her hair or the way she held her lips in a thin line that inspired fear into the hearts of her students, but rather the way her sea green eyes would bore into their souls or at least it seemed that way.

"Muir, don't fail me now," Zinnia whispered to the god of the sea. She turned just in time to see the balcony with the Royal guests. This test was a public display, as it was the intention of rewarding those with the strongest magic in their veins. To not only reward but to recognize that they still held true to the magic that Muir had woven through their beings. Those of the royal family were always invited. Zinnia blinked and turned to look down at her Mistress once again.

"Prince Loch and Prince Ruari are in attendance, so is Lady Thetis," Dru motioned toward the top balcony. "Some would say it is an honor and I say it's nauseating. Nothing like adding more pressure," he murmured as he swiped a hand down his face.

Zinnia opened her mouth to reply, but soon Mistress Oinone began to speak.

"Greetings my lovely students! Congratulations on making it this far into your schooling. We, as Merfolk, pride ourselves in our magic. We are all born with it humming in our veins, but as with those with the affinity to draw or calculate, some have a better grasp of it. I applaud those who are here," she said before she allowed for the audience to applaud.

"It was by no small task that you came to be here. This year we have twelve students who will be partaking in the trial, may you sing true and persevere evermore." Mistress Oinone did not move from her perch, but she did look to the balcony, bowed her head to the royal family and signaled for the first student to move to the podium.

Zinnia watched with rapt attention, the test went alphabetically and as far as names went she happened to be dead last. The first Mer that took to the stage was tested on her vocal scale, magic spun in the current with each note, anyone with enough magic running through them would have felt it. The magic caused the girl's eyes to glow faintly and when she was through with the scale she was allowed one moment to gather herself. Next, it was her physical magic, instead of using her voice to draw the power it came from glyphs which were crafted by her fingers. Symbols were created by simple or complex curling of fingers or flicks of the wrist. Lastly, a scenario was created by the Mistress so that both of these magics would have to be utilized, both required concentration, strength and a fair amount of power to continue through successfully.

Dru shuddered beside Zinnia as he jammed his fingers through his hair. "I don't want to be next," he complained. Calm, cool and collected Dru, who was always so certain of himself looked anything but sure of himself. That was twice now in two days that he looked ready to vomit or at least slip unconscious.

Zinnia leaned against his shoulder and pat his back. "You'll do fine, Dru. You're a brilliant binder," she encouraged him.

And then Mistress called Dru's name.

Dru's test went on without a hitch, she wasn't lying when she said he was a brilliant binder. The glyphs were more akin to woads that etched themselves in the seawater—they were filled with his magic, a visual display of what ran through his veins. His voice was impeccable; deep, lulling and clear. A Mer with magic could create it and weave it with their voice, but they could also perform spells with a series of gestures with their fingers.

Zinnia knew that if things had panned out differently in life she would have thought him to be a fine suitor, he was such a talented witch, and yet, here they were. She could still recognize his beauty for what it was, beauty in looks, heart, soul, and gods! That voice.

When finally it was Zinnia's turn she flexed her fingers and gulped down a mouth of the current. Dru's arms encircled her and his lips touched her cheek.

"May you sing true and persevere evermore," Dru whispered as he allowed for Zinnia to move away.

She closed her dark eyes and swam down toward the staging, it was as if everything had ceased to move. Zinnia cast her eyes to her friend, forced herself to smile and caught the pale blond hair of Prince Loch, the sight of his hair caused her heart to pound violently and she didn't know why.

FIRE WITHIN

"Zinnia, if you may begin your scale, please," Mistress Oinone prompted.

She startled for a moment, torn away from the smiling face of Prince Ruari. Zinnia took a deep breath and opened her mouth. The music poured out in a soprano tone, each note enunciated properly, each note she hung onto. Music saturated the auditorium, everything seemed to fade away as she poured her heart, soul and being into the notes as if her life depended on it.

Around Zinnia, the water seemed to still, the audience quieted and focused wholly on her. She did not simply sing the scale, but she wove each note together and created a beautiful aria. By the time she had completed the song, the trance was broken.

Mistress Oinone did not seem nearly as stunned as everyone else. "And now for your glyphs." She nodded and motioned to continue on.

Zinnia flexed her fingers against one another, touched fingertip to fingertip and glyphs began to glow in the current, floating around in colorful whirls. They built on one another and unlike the other students, the glyphs began to form pictures that moved in an upward column.

The column accumulated as she tapped into the magic she felt surrounding her, it no longer belonged to just Zinnia, it belonged to the others, too. Like a greedy traveler, she drank from them and supplied the column with the energy she gained.

It was done.

Mistress Oinone touched Zinnia's arm to cease her from siphoning the magic, it was taboo, but it was too late.

This wasn't bad, Zinnia knew that every one of them had magic and some had more than others, but not everyone could siphon the energy from within and not everyone could do it without taxing the person.

Why did she feel like there was a giant mark on her then? When she looked up at the balcony once more, Prince Ruari had a crooked smile on his face, Prince Loch had a scowl and Lady Thetis looked fascinated. Zinnia looked to her friend for comfort and it was Dru that began clapping before anyone else.

The trial had ended and only a chosen few would be selected.

"You drew the attention of nearly everyone there, Zin,

I think most would call it unnatural," he said in a teasing tone.

"It is not! It's what happens when the lines are closed off so tightly, instead of flourishing, magic dies." That was the truth and while Dru had meant it as a joke, her mood soured.

The fact was Megalopolis had turned its nose up at the thought of mingling with those from surrounding farm towns and lesser vicinities of Selith, because of this their gene pool had grown smaller and the magic seemed to diminish in their bloodlines.

"Okay, I surrender, you don't need to snap at me. I'd like to point out you managed to ensnare the attention of the royal family, too." He waggled his brows to emphasize this.

It was not her intention to snap at Dru, it wasn't his fault she felt insecure at that moment. Yet, Dru was a rarity, he held more magic in his veins than most of his noble peers combined.

Zinnia swam toward a seat in the waiting room, everyone had sectioned themselves off into the cliques in the academy, it was just her and Dru in this one.

"Tell me what you discovered yesterday," Zinnia prompted and felt her body hum with a mixture of excitement and dread. "In regard to Jager and… the Prince," she whispered so no one could hear.

Dru's lips pressed together and he lowered himself to

"Zinnia's Secret"
by Lou Wilham

a seat. "Not much, but a few of the bystanders overheard some of the shouting. They said Prince Loch had… well, he accused Jager of visiting the Crevice and performing a spell," he paused and tapped his fingers on his forearm.

"How would he even know unless he was there?" Zinnia's face scrunched up in disbelief. She wasn't buying it.

"Well, that's the thing, but apparently there was an incident and outside of that, I don't know." He shrugged his slender shoulders and looked as irritated as Zinnia felt.

She proceeded to tell him her findings, afterward they both fell quiet.

"Miss Zinnia, I presume?" Came a rich, playful tone.

That wasn't Dru teasing her, in fact, it wasn't his voice at all, Zinnia cocked her head as she looked up at the newcomer. Her mouth fell agape at once, dark eyes widened and she all but fumbled out of her seat to allow herself to properly greet a member of the royal family.

"Y-Y-Your Highness! Yes, I am Zinnia," she stammered. Since when did Zinnia stammer? Since never, that was when, yet here she fumbled over her words and had to fight to recall the proper greeting.

"No need for theatrics, I'm not one for all that show." He flashed a toothy grin as he spoke, which only seemed to grow at her discomfort. "That was quite an impressive display earlier, what do you think the chances of winning are?" He inquired, his light blue eyes traced over her features.

Prince Ruari appeared to be genuinely inquisitive as if he truly didn't know who would win and perhaps he didn't. It was Zinnia's way of thinking that the Royal House always knew who would win, that they had a hand in selecting who won. However, she was willing to bet her only jeweled coral piece that he did know and he was teasing her. Leave it to a member of the privileged royal family to taunt an urchin such as herself. Well, at least she had worked her fins off to be here!

"The results are in! They are in!" One of the fellow students shouted as she swam into the room. "They're calling all of the students back to the auditorium, come on!" The girl's face was flushed and her wild blue hair trailed behind her as she fled the room.

Ruari turned his head toward the girl and hummed."Hm, well, I guess we'll find out," he said, as he dipped his head down and grinned broadly. "I hope you sang true and no matter what, may you persevere after this." And with that, he swam back to the auditorium.

"That was different," Dru said as he leaned over Zinnia's shoulder. His blue eyes scanned her face and when it was clear she wasn't about to respond he waved a hand in front of her.

"Why was he just speaking to me?" Zinnia's eyes

widened as her eyes followed the retreating figure of Prince Ruari.

"Maybe he thinks you're pretty," Dru began to talk and coughed as he felt an elbow jab his stomach. "Or maybe he saw your talent for what it was." A groan slid from him as he rubbed his stomach.

Whatever the reason, it was now time to see who had been declared the winner.

Mistress Oinone was no longer seated and in her hand, she held a plaque which had been elaborately designed. On the plaque held the name of the winner, by her side on the seat had the runner-up.

"First things first, I'd like to say everyone did splendidly. There were however two individuals that shone brightly today. The runner-up is… Lord Dru of House Ameria." The crowd broke off into a fit of applause. He was well liked by his community, it was no secret.

Zinnia gasped. "Dru! Oh my gods, congratulations!" She hugged him tightly before she gave him a playful shove toward the stage. She was beyond happy for him and yet she felt a pit grow inside of her. What if the winner wasn't her? This was it, she had to win because if she didn't then she would forever be known as the bottom feeder.

"And, for the moment we have been waiting for… It is with great honor that I present to you the winner, Miss Zinnia of Limnaia!" Mistress Oinone exclaimed.

Zinnia sat rooted to her seat, afraid to move. As if movement would stir her from this dream and yet, she saw Mistress wave her down. She swam quickly and reached for the plaque with her name etched into it. She felt tears prick her dark eyes and it was then she looked up toward the balcony and she caught Prince Ruari with a smug look on his face as he clapped. Beside him, Prince Loch looked disgusted and beside him sat Lady Thetis, who promptly elbowed him in the ribs.

"Congratulations, Zinnia," her Mistress whispered into her ear as she hugged her.

She focused on Mistress Oinone instead of the balcony and nodded her head. "Thank you, Mistress," she whispered and lifted the plaque in her shaking hands.

"No, Zinnia, today we are equals. You are no longer a student, you are now a full-fledged Sea-Witch." Oinone smiled fondly at the young mermaid and motioned for her to turn toward the crowd. "Take your final bow. Tomorrow, you pick your coven."

She turned and took a bow, hands clutched onto the plaque as if someone was going to rip it away from her. The crowd did not roar like it had for Dru and to her amusement, a good portion of them seemed confused, even angrily shocked.

Zinnia couldn't help how her eyes flicked up to the balcony again. Prince Ruari was the only one remaining in the balcony, he leaned against the balcony, his smug expression had vanished and was replaced by a kind, thoughtful look.

In spite of a restless night of sleep Zinnia had done it, she felt shook to the core and overwhelmed by it all, and she cried.

EARTH AROUND

Dru's face was split into a wide grin, his fingers clutching onto the plaque he received. "Your mother is going to be proud, Zinnia," he said as he swam with her toward the exit.

"I am, very proud," Aminta's voice called out as she swam up to Zinnia and embraced her. "So proud and your father would be, too. Oh, Zin, congratulations," she whispered, joy glimmering in her eyes. "I'll see you at home, work calls, oh baby girl… I'm so proud of you." She leaned forward and kissed her daughter.

Emotions welled up inside of Zinnia as she embraced her mother. "Love you, see you later."

Dru smiled and waved to Aminta as she swam off. He

spun around to face Zinnia, his eyes narrowing. "Did you see Loch watching you like a hawk?"

"It was difficult to not notice," she mumbled and shrugged her shoulders. Although, she had wondered why he looked at her as if she were some kind of savage.

"I find it interesting that he was seen hounding a known witch before a Trial *for* witches…" Dru offered as he turned his head away.

Zinnia considered this for a moment and nodded her head. "It would make sense to be fearful of us. It is known that magic is slowly dying out and those who don't have it would be held with suspicion or contempt."

"Maybe he's lacking magic himself," Dru teased as he swam ahead and into the city pathway.

"Now, there is a thought," she said and swam after him, allowing her tail to propel her through the stronger current.

Megalopolis might have been haughty, but Selith was so rigid in its beliefs that even Megalopolis often seemed outlandish in comparison. The old noble blood lived in Selith City, as did the Royals and their opinion of outsiders, anyone not born in the city, was inconsequential.

Alabaster buildings loomed over the pathways, everything about the city screamed prestige and Zinnia smiled, because although she would never truly belong to Selith, she had proved herself worthy.

As she rounded the corner of the pathway with Dru, a cry rang out. Not far from them, a figure with a hood over their head was pushed into the middle of the path.

"You don't belong here!" A Mermaid cried out.

"You are banned from entering the City!" The Merman who had pushed the shrouded individual ground out.

"I am guilty of *nothing*," the voice growled.

Zinnia touched her fingers to her lips, the voice sounded familiar and just as she was piecing together why it sounded so familiar a hand pulled the hood free of the victim.

"If that was even remotely true…" The Merman seethed and raised his fist to strike Jager.

Zinnia rushed forward, unable to stop herself and she raised her plaque to stop the blow. "Stop! Stop at once! He says he is not guilty!"

Dru crept forward toward Zinnia and used his body to shield Jager, too.

The Merman seemed to recognize Dru, he made no attempts to shield his disappointment in the boy, it radiated from him.

"He is guilty of far more than you children know, go home and let us deal with him." There was no room for argument or at least there wouldn't have been if it hadn't been Zinnia and Dru.

"Let him speak," said the Mermaid who had screeched

at him before. "Let's see what he has to say." She nodded and folded her arms across her bejeweled dress.

Jager scowled at the back of Zinnia and Dru's head before pushing his way forward. "I was here *healing* one of your own. You can ask Zebar if you'd like, now if that is it, I have a shop to run." He bit his words out and raised his brows as if challenging anyone to say otherwise.

Zinnia watched as left, she clutched the plaque to her chest and looked at Dru. Everyone was beginning to move on except the Mer who had nearly struck Jager.

"They should outlaw magic, your kind cannot be trusted." His eyes moved to the plaques in their grasp and he sneered. "One day and not a day too soon, you will all be shunned. There is no place for magic here." He swatted at the current and swam away.

"Come on, Dru, let's go, we're going to..." Zinnia began.

"Let me guess, pester Jager until he binds us to the Capitol building for a week?"

Zinnia snorted. "No, well, yes, but hopefully not the latter," she teased and raced down the path.

By the time they caught up with Jager, he had already crossed into Megalopolis again. He swam with a purpose and Merfolk parted for him with ease. He turned around once and noticed the pair following him and shook his head.

"What do you kids want?" he asked gruffly.

"I just want to know why they hate you, why Prince Loch…" she began and bit her bottom lip.

Jager's eyes took note of the plaques in their grasp for the first time. His dark blue eyes focused on them before he gestured at them. "I'd say congratulations, but I'm afraid this is not the time for our kind. It would seem that Selith is not only keen on keeping its old traditions, but grudges, too."

What was she to say to that? She knew that for a fact. She shrugged her shoulders and continued on, unperturbed by his gruffness. "Thank you. I know about your brother and what happened centuries ago," Zinnia began and was surprised when her wrist was snatched up in Jager's grasp.

His grip was strong and unforgiving. Dru hurried up to him and pushed at his chest, ready to use his plaque as a weapon if need be.

Jager sneered at him and laughed, there was no humor in his gaze. "Don't speak of what you don't know a damn thing about, kid. You know nothing about my brother." His grip softened around her wrist but he didn't let go, even with Dru in his face.

"Let her go." Dru gave him another way out, but if he didn't relent, another scene was going to go down in front of Jager's shop.

"Get inside, the both of you." He released Zinnia's wrist and jerked his head toward the inside.

They complied and filed inside.

Jager's shop was full of artifacts that had tumbled into the sea over the past several centuries. They belonged to the Uplanders, some were quite beautiful and others simply strange, but most knew that this was only a front. Jager dealt in magic first and foremost, his shop was his side business.

"You kids don't belong snooping around. I know you're witches, but you don't understand. You're going to get hurt, so let it go. My brother died because of magic and it killed other Mer, too." He sounded less angry when he spoke this time, his face looked fairly drained.

"And you still practice it, so it isn't that bad," Dru offered.

"I didn't say it was bad, look, you're about to choose your Coven, right?"

They both nodded their heads at his question.

"Alright, my advice? Listen to your Coven leader, period. No heroics, no dabbling in anything you shouldn't, just listen to what you're told. You seem like bright kids. Alright? Go, I have work to do."

Zinnia's mouth gaped open, she struggled to find the

words to say. There were so many questions she had but Dru pulled her by the elbow and they left Jager's shop.

"That was enlightening." A snort came from him.

"Yeah, if you say so." Zinnia was still so confused.

As they swam along, the seafloor began to quake, cracks formed in the basins and some of the buildings began to groan. Screams swarmed the current and the building closest to where they tread began to crumble.

A young mother and her child tried to swim away, but it was no use.

"No!" Zinnia ditched the plaque in her grasp and held up her hands as she belted a note of magic. The current caused by it pushed the piece of the building away from them and thudded to the ground.

Just as quickly as the quake began it ceased, destruction was left in its path and not for the first time did Zinnia feel uneasy.

Panicked, Zinnia looked around for Dru, he was nowhere to be seen but his voice caught her attention down the pathway. Relieved, she swam after him.

"Are you okay?" she asked hurriedly.

"Yes, are you?" His eyes swept along her figure to assess her.

"What the depths was that?" She looked around. The buildings around her had remained standing, for the most part. Some had giant cracks in them, just the one across the way had toppled.

"He's fighting the binding, he's trying to break free," a voice said behind Zinnia.

She spun around to face Jager, who looked pale and drawn. "Who?" she inquired with wide eyes.

"My brother."

Zinnia paled and swam closer to him. "What do you mean your brother?" She pressed him for more information.

"Kriegen, the one everyone knows as Kraken," he offered in a whisper. "It's what Prince Loch accused me of. I was at the Crevice, but I was *binding* him. I've felt him tugging at his restraints, but none have listened to me."

Everything in Zinnia froze and she couldn't help but gape at him. From the rumors to the history she had read it certainly made sense, but to hear it from Jager's mouth was another thing entirely.

"He's your brother?" Dru's voice climbed an octave as he stared at him.

Jager ran a hand down his face and swam by the two. "We have to head to the palace. You," he said and motioned toward Dru. "Go alert the Coven, we will be at the palace, but tell Oinone to gather at the pillars and wait for me."

Zinnia gave Dru a brief hug and swam after Jager. By the time she reached his side she was panting softly, gods he could swim.

"What are we going to do at the palace? Prince Loch isn't fond of you," she whispered and almost regretted it instantly.

Jager pinned her with a glare. "For something I didn't do and was not responsible for. I was never my brother's keeper and by the time I realized how hungry for power he had become it was too late. His greed and determination to keep the Uplander's at bay corrupted him. The magic he called on was not of *our* magic, what we as witches of the sea represent.

"I wasn't there, not when he conjured up the darkness. I was gathering up another coven and by the time I returned Kriegen's black magic had consumed the witches, the warriors and anyone who was around him. The only thing I was able to do was bind him to the crevice with my magic. As far as I'm concerned, my brother died that day." Jager continued to swim until he reached his shop, behind it was his carriage and he was quick to hook his Hippocampus up.

With a nod of his head, he motioned to it. "Climb in."

Zinnia did just that and nestled into the cushioned seat. A snap of the reins and they were off to the palace.

METAL BINDS

Before them loomed the Great Palace, it was even more

impressive up close; a porcelain structure with golden accents. The gates to it were golden, guarded heavily by soldiers and when they saw the approaching carriage the guards moved their swords across their body in a defensive stance.

"Halt," the nearest one called out.

Jager moved from the carriage before Zinnia and helped her out. "We have urgent news that must be passed to the King."

"Do you have an appointment?" his tone was shrewd.

"No, I assure you this is important," Jager argued back, he didn't shrink or look away, his gaze remained squarely on the guard.

"Go away, bottom feeders." He turned his back to them in refusal.

"Open the gates, this is urgent!" Jager's composure melted, he shouted at the guard which did nothing to dissuade him.

Zinnia felt helpless, but she noticed a flash of red hair in the courtyard, the familiar teal and emerald tail…

"Your Highness!" she cried out and moved toward the gates. She pressed her face against the bars and wrapped her fingers around it, praying to whatever gods that would listen.

Prince Ruari turned his head to face her, he swam up to her quickly and furrowed his brows. "Zinnia? What brings…" his words died off as his gaze swept to Jager.

The smile that had been forming on his face froze and he swallowed.

"Jager, you being here means nothing good." His shoulders sagged as he nodded to the guard to open the gates.

Hesitantly, the guard did just that and allowed for them to pass through.

"I'm afraid not, Kriegen is breaking loose." Jager didn't mince words, he cut to the chase and it had the desired effect.

Zinnia interjected, "the quake, you felt it? It was worse in Megalopolis." Quakes happened from time to time, but never that severely and judging by the structures they had seen on the way it hardly touched Selith City, Zinnia thought it was due to the proximity of the crevice to Megalopolis.

"… Follow me now." Ruari blanched, his hand swept through his hair and he began to race toward the palace's doors. "Save whatever you have to say for my father." As the doors opened he swam through with Zinnia and Jager flanking him.

"Where is my father?" Ruari questioned a servant, the stern look on his face looked quite out of place on his face. The jovial, twinkle in his eye was gone and replaced with worry and intensity.

This was not lost on Zinnia, but she remained quiet and if there had not been such a pressing matter at hand she likely would have gawked at the palace. This was the first time she had been here, but at the moment she was focused on the task at hand.

"Your Highness, His Majesty is meeting with the council," a servant began.

"Good enough," Ruari replied and rushed through the hall toward the meeting room.

No one was there to stop them as he pushed open the doors, Ruari burst in with a rush of energy and lifted a hand. Zinnia and Jager followed suit behind, she may have felt out of place but Ruari was at home and Jager looked intense.

King Eidir and Prince Loch sat at the head of the meeting table, their blue eyes widened in shock. "What is the meaning of this, Ruari? You better have a good reason for bursting in here like that with..." His aged eyes flicked to Jager, lips pursed in thinly veiled disgust.

"It is urgent, I'll apologize for the intrusion after," he began. "The binding is loosening on the Kraken. There was a quake reported in Megalopolis."

"That's absurd, Ruari," Loch groused. He placed his hands on the table as he rose from the high-backed chair. "Is this some joke? Something you and your little friends have conjured up?" He eyed his brother dubiously, but it was the King who replied.

"Loch, let your brother have his words," There was no room left for argument.

"Word has been sent to Oinone, who will no doubt contact the other covens. This shouldn't be brushed aside, even if it turns out to be nothing would it not best to be safe rather than sorry?" Ruari implored, his gaze focused on his father.

"Your Majesty, with all due respect, *Kriegen* was once and I suppose still is part of my blood. I felt a flux of magic, familiar magic at the time of the quake." It was Jager who spoke and caused the room to become disgruntled.

Zinnia fidgeted, the council eyed Jager like he was a parasite to be squashed. She, on the other hand, didn't seem to exist.

"Your Majesty, you cannot take this seriously. That creature has been bound away for centuries," one of the elders dared to speak out. His wrinkled face a mask of distaste and frustration.

"I second that," another one of the councilmen said.

"Silence, I trust my son. Before this gets out of hand, ensure that the coven looks into it and I'll send out a small fleet of soldiers." He rapped his fingers on the table and looked to Loch, who was not impressed and looked quite red in the face.

"Loch, go with Ruari," he motioned with his hand. "We will part at once," he sighed and looked to the council. "This meeting is adjourned for now, until this situation is handled.." With a nod of the head, he excused himself.

When the room emptied Loch approached Ruari and Zinnia, his eyes bore into her before he looked to his brother. His severe lips pressed into a thin line and proud brows drew in. "I will never understand you or father's love for magic. It begs for darkness and greed," he gave Zinnia a meaningful glance before he jerked his head to the door. "Let us go and be done with this." With that, Loch was out the door, too.

"Don't mind him, he's perpetually rankled." Ruari teased in light of the situation.

"He hates me," Zinnia stated, not looking affronted in the least. She recalled the glare he offered her during the trial and it seems his hatred hadn't lessened any.

"No, he hates Jager," he chuckled and eyed Jager. "If we were not brothers I daresay he'd feel the same way about me, as it is, he isn't a fan of what I have and he doesn't."

"But he will be King one day," Zinnia offered and in return Jager snorted.

Ruari's head reared back and he shrugged a shoulder. "True, but is a title everything? You ought to know." He didn't say it in a harsh way, but it still stung.

In the hallway, Prince Loch approached, a deep blue tail propelled him and the severity of his gaze was not lost on Zinnia. "Two carriages await, let's go."

"Before we leave, *Your Highness,* we will be meeting with the Coven at the pillars, *then* the crevice." Jager's gaze challenged the Prince, but no argument poured from him. Not even a scolding.

The carriages waited and the small group of soldiers had gathered before the drivers called out their departure.

"King Eidir wishes to down play this, but keep your wits about you, Zinnia. This is not a joke, it is not something to be taken lightly. Kriegen has become a monster and won't hesitate to kill you." Jager pinched the bridge of his nose in frustration.

As the carriage pulled to a stop in front of the circle of pillars, Oinone approached and clasped her hands in front of her. "Jager," she called out, her green eyes searched the window.

"Oinone," he bowed his head and moved toward her. "He told you, then?" Jager's eyes flicked toward Dru.

"Dru told me, we've assembled and are ready. Jager… we won't be able to fight him, not this time. We need more *time,*" she paused.

"More witches, I think you mean. What are swords and tridents against magic?" he whispered viciously.

Oinone glanced at her prior students. "Be careful today, this is no trial."

Once the Coven was fully assembled, the entourage of soldiers and witches alike went forth to the Crevice. None were prepared for what they saw. A collective gasp rang out and the younger Mer let shrieks of terror escape.

The Crevice had split open, black, tar-like bubbles escaped and tendrils of the same black liquid snaked through the water. Tendrils, or rather tentacles, slapped down on the seafloor, and a booming cackle of laughter emitted through the current.

The soldiers had long since spilled onto the scene, abandoning their hippocampus as they held up their shields and weapons. In return, the Kraken's bindings snapped and allowed him to emerge fully from his prison.

His voice hummed through the current. "Brother, you came," his voice rumbled as his immense form slithered across the seafloor. Kriegen loomed just above his brother.

"You knew I would," he shouted.

One of his tentacles shapeshifted into a blackened hand and it swiped through the current. "Yes, I suppose I did," he sneered, his distorted features no longer resembled that of a Mer and not quite a beast, either. "I would have been disappointed had you not." The seafloor trembled, sending new cracks spreading along the crevice edge. A groan sounded as it tore open wider.

Zinnia gasped, Dru gripped her hand and used his shoulder to steady her. She wanted to flee, wanted to be far from the fight because they didn't belong here or did they? They had not taken up their vows with a coven, but they would be sworn to protect their kingdom and people.

The sound of Loch's voice tore Zinnia's attention from Kriegen, he had his body turned away and he was shouting. The King pushed his way through the crowd, golden plated armor covered his body and a helm shielded his face. He had taken it far more seriously than what was believed.

"*Your Majesty*," Kriegen hissed and let his appendages ripple and pull him closer. With every movement, the seafloor shuddered and the current seemed to be deprived of oxygen.

"Kriegen!" Jager shouted, his brother turned to him for a moment, considering him.

To the side, King Eidir advanced, there was nothing he could do to physically harm the monster, but he would lead his people. "It is time to do away with you, once and for all!" Eidir shouted.

The monster paid little attention to the King, but in a lightning fast maneuver, Kriegen whipped out a tentacle, slapped it down onto the King and not one, but two more tentacles followed suit. A hiss of laughter erupted from Kriegen as he pulled his blackened limbs back to reveal a lifeless King Eidir.

Zinnia shrieked and Dru reeled her toward his side as Oinone came up to them.

"Come, we all need to be together, have heart. Together we are stronger, we need to bind him back to the crevice." Oinone pulled them off to where the other witches gathered, they joined hands and began to hum. Together, their voices united and built nearly tangible notes in the water. Thick cords of magic billowed in the current, growing and growing.

Chaos erupted, Zinnia felt her hand squeezed and when she looked up it was Prince Ruari. His pale cheeks flushed with color and his blue eyes sparked with a new intensity; one that she recognized as grim determination.

Nothing could be said to him at that moment, she knew the loss of a parent and instead she threaded her hand with his and allowed for her body to rest against his, too. Prince or not, he grieved just the same as any other.

The battle raged on, the distraction the soldiers provided didn't last long, there were too few of them and Kriegen's rage gave him strength. Too long he had been shackled to the depths. His shriek boomed through the air as his tentacle slapped down on the last soldiers that were left.

Kriegen loomed above the coven and his limbs struck down once more, his body slithered closer to the coven. His mouth contorted into a vicious grin and with a strike, he disrupted the coven's circle.

A sound burst from his mouth, a note, and Zinnia realized it was a spell. He was beginning to cast a spell!

They could all die.

Zinnia's tears melded with the sea water, the blood of the coven began to ooze into the water around them. A sob lodged itself in Zinnia's throat but as much as she wanted to curl in on herself she pulled herself together. She swam off and motioned toward the rest of the coven, Kriegen's attention had been pulled away.

Jager swam toward his brother, calling to the god of the sea, calling upon every cell of his magical makeup so that he could bind his brother. Little by little Kriegen's appendages seemed to still and the floor groaned as it began to seal. His contorted figure seemed to shrink but he was not without a fight, some bindings snapped and caused shockwaves to ripple through the sea.

The coven continued to work, but it was Zinnia who pulled away from the circle and swam a distance behind the thrashing beast. A song poured from within as she lifted her hands and began to weave magic in the current. She allowed herself to focus on the hum, ignored the thunderous growl of Kriegen as he spun around to face the maid who dared defy him.

Perhaps it wasn't the brightest of ideas, but the strands of her magic lashed against him and caused him to flinch, but in turn, it allowed for the coven to weave their bindings more efficiently, too.

A curse escaped Jager, but he kept chanting his spell and circled his hand in the water to create a thick tendril of magic and then did the same before he launched them forward at Kriegen.

Oinone pulled her hands free and the rest of the coven did the same and as they pushed their hands forward they all released a band of bindings. Kriegen was slapped in several directions by the invisible chains and his limbs began to buckle.

A sickening crack filled the current as the crevice groaned in dismay, Kriegen's body began to bend and collapse beneath the bindings.

Neither Jager nor Zinnia or the coven relented.

In one last effort, Kriegen began to slap his tentacles down in an attempt to crush as many as he could, the pull of the bindings began to yank him back into the deep. He howled in fury and lashed out, one tentacle fell heavily on a part of the circle.

"Don't stop, Zinnia!" Jager cried out and averted his gaze from Kriegen to the fallen coven members. There was less magic flowing forth, but the bindings had begun to latch onto the monster.

She didn't stop, as much as she may have wanted to she kept her focus on trapping the beast.

One last cry emitted from the Kraken before his body was swallowed up by his prison once again and it wouldn't be the last.

In spite of the temporary victory, no one cheered. Bodies littered the seafloor, blood coursed through the current. The reality slammed through everyone, the King had been killed today.

A week had passed since the battle between Mer and Kriegen.

Since the incident, Prince Loch shut down the teachings of magic at the Academy. He didn't outlaw magic, but he certainly didn't make it easy for a Mer to be taught. There was still such contempt in his gaze when it came to witches and for the first time, he couldn't be blamed for that.

"We need to move forward, away from magic. The Dark Arts are far too enticing, if it is harder to come by the knowledge then it will be equally as difficult to find trouble," Prince Loch had declared at a formal meeting.

Zinnia had been there, alongside Dru and Jager, she still couldn't believe how swiftly the events had occurred but she knew for certain that she would not refrain from practicing magic, she knew Dru wouldn't cease either.

"From here we will plan and be ready for the Kraken when he breaks loose again because the next time there won't be any more binding." Prince Ruari looked at Jager as he said this.

"No, you're right. The next time he perishes," Jager folded his hands and sat back.

Once they were all in agreement, Zinnia swam into the hall and steeled herself. She felt rather than saw a presence by her side, one flick of the tail and she knew who it was.

In spite of the weight of the moment, she felt a smile tug at her lips and then surprise washed over her dark gaze when the figure lifted her hand.

"I will see you around, Zinnia, our work is not yet finished," Prince Ruari's lips teased the back of her hand and he gave her a roguish smile.

He swam away and left her gaping down at her hand. A small blush colored her cheeks.

"And I still find this interesting," Dru offered and chuckled.

Zinnia had not heard him and she startled before a laugh escaped.

"So do I." She smiled.

About Elle Beaumont

Elle was born and raised in Southeastern, Massachusetts in a little farm town by the harbor. She grew up fascinated with all things whimsical and a strong love for animals.

As she grew so did her passion for reading and writing. Although she prefers devouring all genres she largely enjoys dark fantasy.

She is married to her best friend and has two lively

sprites who inspire madness, love and a sense of humor in her. They also have a menagerie of animals, two dogs, three cats and a horse. In her downtime, Elle enjoys creating candles, crocheting, horseback riding and running.

CONNECT ON SOCIAL MEDIA

facebook.com/ellebeaumontbooks

instagram.com/ellebeaumontbooks

The Sinking

K.M. Robinson

THE CHIMES JINGLE AS THE PAWNSHOP DOOR CLOSES. I probably shouldn't have sold them, but mother says I need to stop hoarding the merchandise.

The shop is usually quiet this time of day, the mothers all picking their children up from school, the men still at their jobs and unable to get off early and come trade two week's worth of pay for a ring for a pretty girl, and the old men that come looking to flirt are still at their late lunches.

I regret giving away the chimes instantly. They're made of metal bars and little seashells—I could easily make another—but I don't like giving my treasures away.

At least the older woman paid extra for it.

I walk away from the register, rifling through my bag on the floor. I look up as the door clicks opens—I was right, I shouldn't have sold the chimes.

Before I can straighten, a woman hovers in front of

me on the opposite side of the counter. She smiles a toothy grin at me.

"I'd like to trade this," she says, holding out a necklace.

I hold out my hand, allowing her to rest the shell in it. Lifting it up, I examine the golden detail work around the metallic shell. The bottom opens, revealing a storage space, though nothing resides inside the shell.

"Legend says, if you dip it into the sea and call out to the waves, it will turn you into a mermaid," she informs me. "If you find your love below the waves, you get to stay, but if you don't, you drown beneath the waves."

"Why are you pawning this?" I ask, closing the bottom of the necklace.

We're not required to ask why people part with their things, but I have nothing better to do while trapped in the tiny shop on the pier. She looks at me thoughtfully.

"My son is in need," she says. "I'll get it back if it doesn't work out."

"I can give you fifty dollars for this," I inform her after examining it—the gold alone is worth more.

"All right," she says, ducking her head. She quietly accepts the money form me.

I push the cash register closed as she heads toward the door.

"You have until the twenty-first to come back for this, ma'am," I call after her.

"Thank you, anemone," she calls back. "Feel free to

wear it until then—it would look beautiful on you. You can even try it in the water if you want to see a little magic."

She winks, turning back toward the door as she fans the ten-dollar bills out that I gave her.

"Try it on now," she insists, spinning back to me, nearly toppling the hair piled on her head under her wrap. "I'd love to see it on you."

I try to refuse but finally give in when she lingers in the doorway, waiting, a wrinkled hand on the doorframe. I clasp it around my neck, allowing her to see the gold piece rest on my collarbone.

As she exits, an older man walks in, looking for nothing in particular other than to spend a few minutes trying to make a pass at me. I show him a few things that recently became available but, inevitably, he turns them all down and leaves empty-handed.

By the time things slow down, the sun is setting over the horizon, casting marvelous colors out onto the ocean's surface. I lock the shop up for the night and wander down the pier.

Slipping my shoes off, I walk through the sand at the water's edge. One of the benefits of living near the ocean is walking in the waves every night after the tourists have gone home—that and perfect beach hair every single day.

I make it all the way to the next pier before I realize I left the necklace on accidentally. My fingers clutch at it, the metal feeling cool in the front and warm where it had rested against my skin.

I sigh, not wanting to walk all the way back to the shop.

"I'll just take it back tomorrow," I mumble to myself.

I try to tuck it under the collar of my shirt, but as I move it, the clasp slips—I must not have closed it all the way. The necklace topples down the front of my chest, bouncing off my body. I scramble to catch it as a wave washes up, but I miss it in the air.

It drops into the wave, tumbling back with it toward the open sea.

"No," I shout, racing toward it.

I try three times to snatch it out of the water before I finally get my fingers around it. A wave crashes against me, knocking my feet out from under me, forcing me to drop my shoes as I fall into the water.

The ocean pulls me away from the shore, crashing me into the sand. I tumble over and over, slamming into the gritty sand under the water. My mouth fills with water and sand, and I try to catch a breath of air as I flip around.

Panic sets in when I realize I won't be able to reach the surface—I don't even know which way is up.

The hands around me do though.

Propelling us through the water, my savior races us toward the surface. I let him guide me, not even bothering to help kick. His movements are swift and purposeful—I cling to his arms as he rescues me.

When I open my eyes, I can breathe again, but the world around me isn't the gold tones of sunset along the sandy beach—it's blue.

"You're fine," he says to me. "Just stay calm, and I'll explain."

I suck in another breath, miraculously not drowning. My eyes grow wide as I watch the man who rescued me float in the water, breathing normally as if he weren't surrounded by ocean.

My eyes trail down his beaded hair, covered in shells, to his chest. A belt sits on his waist, covered in bits of fish scales.

"I'm Quay," he informs me. My eyes dart back up to his face. "I'm sure this must be strange to you, but you're safe here. I'll help you."

His hands circle around my wrists as I tread water. He moves slightly, mimicking my motions to stay put in the ocean. Except…he's not moving like I am. The man is moving his hips back and forth with one motion instead of two as if walking on a treadmill.

I glance down again, reevaluating my situation—those weren't fish scales on a belt—it was a tail.

Quay has a tail.

I clench my teeth together as I force my eyes to keep dropping until I can see my own tail.

My white and gray print dress with the beautiful, luxurious sleeves is gone. My belt has washed away in the current and been replaced with a tail.

"Look at me," Quay squeezes my wrists as I begin to panic. "Tell me your name."

"Cara."

"Cara, look at me," he replies. When I don't, his hand darts up, catching my chin until I meet his ice-blue eyes. "You were pulled into the sea. You've been given a gift."

"A tail?" I ask in horror.

"You would have died in the water today had the sea not taken pity on you," he informs me. "You were transformed into a mermaid so that you would survive—you've been found worthy, Cara."

He drops his hand, leaving my face feeling exposed.

"Come, I have much to show you." He turns to swim away, still holding my wrist in one hand. "I'm bringing you to my mother—she's the queen of this part of the sea—she'll be able to explain this to you better."

"I need to get my legs back. I have to go home."

"Yes, the queen will help you." I find it curious that he refers to his mother by her title, but I don't say anything.

He smiles softly, nodding to get me moving. His eyes are narrow, but long—almost cat-like.

I follow along quietly, figuring out how to use my tail as he moves us along. I don't know which way land is, but

I imagine we're swimming further and further away from it.

I'm grateful I left my laptop at home today—it would be destroyed at this point. As it is, I'll need a new cell phone now. At least I didn't have any money on me—just the debit card I got a few months ago when I opened my bank account to start saving for a car to take to college next fall.

Fish swim all around us as we dive deeper in the water. I start to realize just how similar we look when a lionfish darts by me.

"You make a lovely mermaid, by the way," Quay looks back, admiring my new body. I blink, unsure of what to say.

His tail is similar to mine, covered in stripes and leafy parts. He almost looks like he found several giant blue beta fish and sewed their tails onto his. A few spikes stick up off the back of his tail, and I reach behind me to examine my own tail—I look like a human-sized lionfish.

I'm incredibly grateful for the sports bra I wore today, though it stands out in stark contrast to the more muted colors of my tail—no way of hiding this, I suppose.

He notices me frowning.

"Would you like some seaweed?" he asks.

"What?" I ask as he stops to face me. He refuses to take his eyes off mine.

"I noticed you looking at your attire. Perhaps it is not

to your liking? I offered you seaweed as a way to change your *iluse*."

"*Iluse*?" I ask, wondering if I'd have an easier time talking to a dolphin.

He motions to my chest without looking down.

"Oh," I catch on. "Oh! Yes, I would like seaweed."

Anything to cover up would be helpful.

Quay guides us further down in the water toward a seaweed garden. He lets me float while he gathers an armful of the water plants for me. The merman drapes them over his forearm, letting each piece have its own resting place. He hovers by my side, holding it out to me, facing the same direction I am to give me space.

I mumble something as I take them and quickly tuck the pieces in and around my sports bra to conceal it while he stares into the distance at my side—wearing light colors to match my dress turned out to not be so helpful today. I wrap pieces around me as low as I can go and still have it tucked into the wire around my bra as I bat my curly hair back.

I didn't realize it was possible to have a bad hair day while floating under the ocean—so much for mermaid hair being perfect.

"So this is an *iluse,* huh?" I ask when I'm done.

"Yes, mermaid," he addresses me. "Are you ready to go?"

This time, he lets me swim on my own, following

along beside him.

"Quay, I can't be a mermaid," I blurt out.

"What do you mean? You're doing splendidly."

"I have to return to the surface," I say, squishing my childhood dreams.

"You have business beneath the sea, Cara," he looks back at me. "You're here for a reason. Shouldn't you explore what that is?"

He looks at me curiously.

"It's not right to waste a gift," he informs me.

"Destroying my cell phone is a gift all of a sudden?"

He furrows his brow when I mention my phone.

"A what?" he questions, nose wrinkled.

"Cell phone," I inform him. "It's a device you call people on—a way to communicate."

"Like a conch?"

"Umm, not exactly." *What?*

"Then what is this device?"

I explain how a cell phone works to the dark merman. I consider fishing it out of my bag to show him, but with my luck, I'd drop it to the bottom of the sea and never be able to find it again…not that it will work, even if I *do* get out of the ocean.

"So exactly like a conch," he replies. "You whisper a name into it, and then the message, and the shell locks out everyone else until it's delivered to the right person. Then your words fizzle away like seafoam."

I'd have to remember that next time I'm collecting shells on my walk home from work.

"Cara, look!" Quay shouts, swimming up in the water.

He bends his fingers so that his body waves as he moves. I push hard on my tail, trying to keep up. I tip my fingers up and down like I did as a child when my dad drove me home from school on his day off, and I stuck my fingers out of the window. I bounce mercilessly in the water until I hold my fingers straight.

"Look here," he says pointing to a tiny sea turtle.

He moves his hand near it, dropping a chain down so that it looks like the small creature was wearing it. Quay lifts it away as stealthily as a magician.

"Is that my necklace?" I gasp. "I was trying to catch it when I fell in."

"It's not yours, Cara," he grins. "Yours is around your neck. I slipped it on when I caught you."

He swims closer to me as my hand flies to my throat.

"This one is mine. It's an octopus, see?" Quay cocks an eyebrow at me. "It's a similar shape though, so I see how you could mistake it."

I'm impressed that he managed to get it around my neck without me noticing. Of course, I was rolling around in a rip tide, so that might have something to do with it.

"I also thought you might like to see the baby turtle."

"It was adorable," I reply, eyes roaming behind him to

see where the creature swam off to, but I have no luck finding it.

"Come, there are more of them near the palace. Is there anything else you would like to see along the way?"

I'm not here for a sightseeing adventure. I'm here to meet the queen and see if she can help me get my legs back.

Then again, the pod of dolphins swimming toward us could make for a cool experience.

"What about them?" I ask, pointing toward the dolphins.

Silently, he swims ahead. I follow as closely as I dare. For a second, I consider catching a ride on his tail but then I realize he's a merman, not a dolphin.

The pod surrounds us, chattering. Quay nods to me as he holds out a hand, allowing a dolphin to slip under his waiting fingers. The moment a gray dorsal fin passes by, he takes off, darting through the water.

A dolphin swims my way. When I was younger, I had the chance to swim with them on vacation once, so I reach out, prepared to catch a ride. The dolphin playfully races through the water, following Quay and it's friend.

Take me to the surface, I will it.

As if reading my mind, we dart up. I squint my eyes closed as we hit the top of the ocean, breaking into the fresh air. The dolphin carries me a few feet before going under the waves.

"Again," I say, encouraging it to surface one more time.

Obliging, we bounce back to the world I know and I look around as quickly as I can.

Land.

I can't reach it though. Not like this. Even if I did, I'd still have fins, so the sea queen is my best bet.

We dive back under the water, swimming low to the ground. If I had feet, I could have skidded to a stop like a parachuter running along the ground after jumping out of a plane.

Quay looks winded when I finally let go of the dolphin, allowing it to join its pod again.

"Are you okay?" I ask, concerned that my guide might pass out on the ocean floor.

"Fine, Cara. How was your swim with Maladai?" He rests a hand on his chest, offering me a weak grin.

"How far did you say the palace is?" I ask skeptically.

"Not too far," he replies. "Shall we continue?"

I nod, letting him guide me again. We swim slower to accommodate him for a few minutes.

"Do you swim with dolphins often?"

"Only when I have to get somewhere quickly. They're much faster than mer are."

We swim for a while in silence. The seaweed ripples under us. Stretching my hand out, I let it dance on my skin, tickling my palm.

"Ah, we have a visitor," Quay murmurs as a group of small mer children swim toward us.

"Prince Quay!" they shout as we draw near. They look shocked and thrilled to see the prince.

Several of them collide with him, slamming into his chest and wrapping themselves around his tail. His laughter is deep and melodic.

"What are you doing here?" an older girl I assume is their sister or babysitter asks. She looks at me critically. Tipping her head toward him, she mumbles. "Should you be out here?"

I smile at the children as they stare at me curiously.

"This is my new friend, Cara. She's from the surface and I'm bringing her to my mother to help her get her legs back," he stresses the words, carefully pronouncing everything.

"She's a human?" the girl's face lights up. She turns to me, smiling. She nods. "Well, we're very pleased to see you."

"Thank you?" I pose my response as a question. *I think.*

She looks like she wants to swim over and shake my hand. Instead, she puts her hand on Quay's strong upper arm.

"Prince Quay will take very good care of you, I'm sure." She turns back to the group of mer children. "Come along, we need to let the prince do his job now."

"But Maianda!" they protest as she quickly turns them around and pushes them forward.

"Not another word," she says bitingly. "We're not disturbing the prince on his birthday."

"It's your birthday?" I ask, turning to him. He looks less strained now as he begins to swim again.

He smiles softly, glancing down.

"It is."

"How old are you?" I ask, expecting some number that's incredibly high.

"Eighteen," he replies as we swim. The children jabber about him in the background, but I don't catch their words, other than *needs to find a human.*

"That's it?" I instantly reply, shocked. I nearly reach up to cover my mouth when I realize I just blurted that out. He chuckles at me.

"What were you expecting me to say, Cara?"

"I don't know," I try not to blush. "All the stories I've heard say that mermaids and mermen live to be hundreds of years old. I assumed this was one of those teen vampire situations where you looked my age but were really four hundred twenty.

He turns back to me, shock written across his face.

"I was clearly born into the wrong collection," he smirks at me. "I should have been a vampire...whatever that is."

I would tease him about missing a pop culture

phenomenon, but it's never impressed *me* either.

"How long *do* you live then?" I question, trying to avoid explaining what a vampire is supposed to be—I have a feeling the best explanation I can come up with involves a shark's teeth.

A long pause follows and I wonder if he's recently lost someone. When he finally answers, it sounds like a struggle.

"Most live into their eighties," he replies.

"I'm sorry," I whisper, swimming closer to him. I put my hand on his shoulder. "I didn't mean to bring that up. I lost my grandpa not too long ago, so I know how much it hurts to lose someone."

He takes a deep breath and pats my hand.

"No, Cara, it's fine," he replies. "We're only a few minutes away from the palace now."

I remove my hand from his shoulder, following him as he guides me to his home. It strikes me as funny that I'm so trusting of this merman that I just met. On the surface, I'd never go anywhere with a guy I didn't know.

"There's a starfish down there," Quay changes the conversation. "They say if you wish on it, it will come true."

"Well, in that case, I wish to go home," I pretend to wish on it. "Not that I'm not having a lovely time, I just really need to make it home before my parents get worried."

I'm sure I've already missed dinner. My family is probably out looking for me right now—too bad I can't text them that I'm running late.

"What did you wish for?" I ask.

"I have a birthday wish today that I'm using on everything," he replies. "It's the same thing I wish for every year on my birthday—I'd like another year."

"Always a good request," I giggle. "So what do mermen do to celebrate their birthday under the sea?"

"We usually dress up in our shoulder armor and *sarasas* and spend time with the mer we care about."

"And yet you were randomly near the surface just in time to save me?" I question. I add slyly, "Quay, were you meeting a mermaid up there? Am I keeping you from some secret rendezvous?"

"No, nothing like that." He looks back at me. "I think I was in precisely the right place at the right time. I couldn't have asked for anyone more beautiful to spend my birthday with."

Is he flirting with me?

"I suppose you don't have cake down here," I mumble ridiculously. "And certainly no candles. Do you sing?"

"Sing?" He stops swimming and turns to face me. "Your customs are very strange, Cara. Usually, the entire kingdom celebrates the prince's birthday, but never on the eighteenth—it's a day meant for transition for the royal line."

"Oh? Do you take over for your parents or something? Am I suddenly swimming in a king's presence?"

"I have a test to pass today. We're here," Quay informs me as we swim up over a ridge.

The palace looks like it's been built out of the treasure from a thousand sunken ships. It shines in the light pouring down through the surface of the ocean, reflecting back at me like a watch on the wrist of a man on the bus reading his newspaper without realizing he's blinding everyone each time he turns the page.

"This is where I live," Quay tells me, guiding me through the front door.

Everything inside sparkles as well. Jellyfish sit at the top of the room, glowing. Seahorses hold onto the pieces of seaweed in the corner. A school of fish quietly glides around the entryway.

"Ah, this is my stingray, Matumb." He reaches out his hand, cuddling the stingray. "You may pet him if you like."

I've fed stingrays before at the aquarium. I reach out, touching its velvety skin. He flaps his wings at me playfully. Quay pulls a dead fish out of the pouch attached to his belt and feeds his pet. Patting it on the head, he sends it off.

"Your Highness," a merman soldier appears in front of us. He gives the prince a sharp nod—I assume it's their version of a bow. "Is there anything I can do for you?"

He almost sounds sad as he asks.

"No, my friend. All is well. Would you inform the queen that I have returned and have brought a friend with me that needs to speak to her."

The soldier's eyes light up similarly to the way the mermaid's had out in the open waters. He nods again, swimming back out of the room.

"Come, you should see the palace while you still can," Quay offers me his hand.

The first room we swim into looks to be some kind of parlor. There are holes in the ceiling that allow the light to shine through. I imagine they're magnificent in the moonlight as well.

"What is that?" I ask, pointing to a bumpy chair.

"That's a lounging couch. We sit on it," he explains as if humans stand all the time. "You may try it if you like."

I bite back my remarks and swim over to it, settling myself between two of the bumps.

"No," he laughs. "Well, *yes,* we *do* sit on it like that when there are more than one of us, but *this* is the proper way."

Quay reaches around my back, scooping up my tail. I suck in a breath as he turns my body, spreading me out over the couch so that my head rests on one bump and my tail hangs over the other. It's surprisingly comfortable.

His hands linger on me, resting on my shoulder and what I suppose would be my knees if I still had them.

"More comfortable?" he asks, grinning over me.

"It is. Is this how you sleep down here?"

"We have beds, just like in your stories."

So he does *know that we don't stand all the time.*

A strand of his shell-clad hair falls in front of him, but he doesn't bother to brush it back as he stares.

"You've read our stories?"

"Sleeping girls and princes, girls who forget their feet...I've seen a few from the old books that fell off sailor's ships generations ago."

"You've read Cinderella?" I laugh.

"Do you know any mer tales?" he shakes his head playfully.

Quay taps my tail, prompting me to set it down on the far side of the couch. He swims around it and sits next to me where my tail had been. Leaning in, he rests his elbows and arms on the bump between us. With his chest pressed against his arms, he puts his chin down on his forearms.

I lean back, scooting down in the seat to see him better.

"A few," I say coyly. If he wants to play games, I can play games. We might be on *his* playing field, but I won't let him have home court advantage.

"My mother likes to tell mermaid stories," I say casually. "She still tells them to my baby cousin every time we babysit. My brother and I may be too old, but I always enjoy listening whenever my cousin comes over for the night."

"You have a brother?"

"I do. Are you the only prince, or are there more?" I challenge.

"I had bothers once," he replies, looking away.

Maybe that was why he was sad earlier.

"I'm sorry," I offer. "Brothers are a wonderful thing to have. I wouldn't trade mine for the world."

"It was hard to let them go. I would have traded places with them if I could have."

"How did you lose them?" I hope I'm not overstepping.

"It's a long story. I'll explain later. For now, you should come with me. We need to get you ready to meet the queen—everything is pageantry down here, and your appearance is no exception."

He holds a hand to me, carefully taking mine in his. We swim down the hall to a room filled with accessories.

"This is our guest closet," Quay says, tucking his braids back over his shoulders. "Whenever we have people who don't live in the palace here and an event comes up, they may borrow pieces."

He swims me to a table covered in headpieces. Shells are scattered everywhere. Bits of coral and driftwood mix with shells and pearls, surrounded by netting and crystals.

"Your *iluse* looks fine, but if you'd like one of ours, you're welcome to it." He motions to a rack near the wall. I nearly select one, but then I realize I might not have anywhere to change and I'm definitely not switching bras in front of him.

"This is fine," I mumble demurely. "What are these?"

He squints his eyes playfully at me as I change the subject.

"You may adorn your hair any way you'd like. Pick one out and I'll help you put it on."

My fingers dance over the crystals and shells. I finally pick one out that's got blue crystals mixed with blue and green shells. Quay takes the one I point to and swims behind me. His tail occasionally pulses against mine when he flicks it to stay floating in the same spot.

The shells aren't as heavy as I expect, though that could be because the water makes everything lighter. Once he has it situated, he swims in front of me, examining the placement on my head. He turns, twisting at the waist to pick up several strands of pearls. His abdomen ripples tightly with the movement, muscles moving gracefully.

"A mermaid should always wear pearls," he explains. "They show off her hair."

Quay swims behind me again, working his fingers

"Leafy Sea-Dragon"
by Lauren Richard
laurenrichardart.com

through my hair expertly. I nearly shudder at his touch. I've always loved when people play with my hair, but it's somehow more luxurious underwater.

"You're very good at this," I comment, tipping my head back slightly into his touch.

"All mermen know how to design hair. It is a sign of love and respect to the mermaids in our lives."

That is the most divine thing I've ever heard.

"That's so interesting. On the surface, guys wouldn't be caught dead knowing what a braid is, much less anything else."

"Your men sound like fools," Quay mutters.

I can't say I disagree.

"It's a shame you can't come to the surface and open a shop—you'd clean up!"

"Clean up?" I'm sure he's wrinkling his nose behind me but I can't see him.

"That just means that you'd be very popular and make a lot of money," I explain. "If you opened a shop and did people's hair, you'd do really well for yourself."

"I'd be a king?" he jokes. "Perhaps I should try it."

He weaves the pearls around the crown, dropping them in my hair so they settle above my eyebrows and ears, stretching around to the back. I close my eyes as he works.

"I'm very sorry this happened to you, Cara. You don't deserve this."

"I'll survive," I reply with a smile. I open my eyes. "You and your mother will help me get back and I'll calm my family down. I'm sure they're panicking right now. I honestly hope they didn't find the shoes I dropped though—that would scare them too much."

"Why is that?"

"I dropped them next to the water. I don't want them thinking I drowned or something."

"I see. All done," Quay says, swimming in front of me to examine his work again. His jaw drops when he sees me. "You look like a mer princess, Cara."

My eyebrows shoot up. There's no way.

He sees my disbelief and purses his lips. Swirling his hand in the water, he creates a large bubble. My image reflects back at me—he's right—I look incredible.

Turning, I examine myself like I do when I'm trying on clothes at the mall. The spikes on my tail accent the brown, orange, and red colors of my scales. Everything makes my dark skin pop. My hair retained its curliness and the pearls look incredible as they sit in my flowing locks. I tip my head—same nose, same pouty lips, but my eyes look larger than usual and more pronounced as if my makeup has changed slightly.

I reach out for my reflection, accidentally popping the bubble. It bursts, taking my image with it.

"You look striking," he repeats. "I don't know how the kingdom will let you go—you are a treasure."

He swims closer. His eyes are mesmerizing in that icy blue tone. He gets so close that I could dart forward and kiss him, *which would be awesome* because the *last thing* I need to do right now is fall for a *merman* and then go back to land.

Pull it together, Cara.

"Do all of the mermaids dress like this?" I ask, turning back to the rows of hairpieces on the table behind Quay.

"Most, yes." He swims beside me, running his fingers over the pieces on the table. "You may keep those for as long as you like. They are a gift."

"Oh, no, I couldn't. I'll return them when I go home," I insist. I'd probably never get the shells and pearls untangled from my hair without his help anyway once I hit the open air.

"Really," he counters. "I want you to have them."

"That's very kind of you, Quay."

"Your Highness, your mother is ready to see you," a merman hovers in the doorway.

"Thank you, we'll be right there," Quay says without turning to face the merman. "I must explain things to you, Cara."

I nod, waiting for his instructions. Surely the queen must be as kind as her son, but I hold my breath, waiting for the shoe to drop.

"I will introduce you when we go in. My mother and the others will likely ask you a series of questions—just answer as best as you can. Do not ask anything yourself unless she gives you permission. She will know why you are here and will explain what you need to do."

"All right," I say softly. "She's nice, isn't she?"

"Everyone loves and respects her. She is the most beloved queen the kingdom has seen in a long time," Quay replies. "Come."

I follow Quay through the hallways, staying close by his side. His fingers brush against mine a few times, but he doesn't flinch, so I hold myself still.

Do not kiss a merman, do not kiss a merman, do not kiss a merman.

The throne room is dazzling. We swim in and the room comes to life. A number of mermaids and mermen hover on the right side of the room, watching us enter.

The mer queen sits on a throne that has clearly been brought in from an old sunken ship and must have belonged to the richest sea captain in the world. They've adorned it with shells and crystals. Sea plants grow beneath it in a colorful rainbow.

"Hello, child," the queen says. Her voice is high and airy.

I'm shocked at how young she looks to have a son

turning eighteen. Her hair is long and luxurious, but she has the same cat-eyes Quay has.

I bow my head sharply like I saw the soldiers do earlier, hoping I got their sign of respect correct. When I look up, she's smiling with approval.

"What is your name?"

"Cara, your majesty." It's strange calling someone that if it's not the tabby cat that lives by the pier where I work.

"Cara, where do you come from?"

"Land." I'd give her the name of my coastal town, but that would just lead to a long—and likely confusing—conversation.

"How did you come to be here?" she asks skeptically.

"I dropped a necklace into the ocean by accident. When I was trying to catch it, the waves pulled my feet out and I ended up in the water."

"You have a tail," the queen points out the obvious.

"The woman who gave me the necklace said it had the power to turn me into a mermaid. I didn't believe her, but apparently it was true."

The queen nods to her court with a smile before turning back to me.

"Do you know why you are here, Cara of land?" she asks. Her hair floats in front of her, but it only adds to the majesty of her presence.

Strands of pearls cover her hair—much like mine—but they also stretch from her shoulder armor to the cuffs around her wrists, creating a cape effect. Her crown is made of gold and stretches high above her, sparking as the last of daylight filters through the water. The room seems alive with color, even though it's fading.

"Your son said you could help me return home. I need to get my legs back and return to my family before they become too worried about me."

"I see," she hums.

If she weren't so lovely and gentle looking, the soft way she is speaking might freak me out. She's like some distant queen in a movie that is removed from her subjects in the storyline but can destroy them all with a single word—I'm shocked she isn't glowing.

"You are here for a purpose, Cara of land," the queen addresses me. "I need you to help me complete a task for my son. Help him and I'll see to it that you make it back to land when it's all over so your parents can find you."

"Anything, your majesty. I just want to go home."

"Very good," the queen nods. She calls her son. "Quay."

He swims closer to me, his energy electric. He seems almost nervous.

"Yes?" she asks her son vaguely.

"Yes, mother," he nearly cringes next to me. His tail flicks impatiently in the water as his fingers close in on his palms.

"We must begin the ceremony immediately," the queen addresses the room, smiling.

"Ceremony?" I ask. Quay looks at me, scared—I spoke when I wasn't supposed to.

"Yes, dear, it's my son's birthday. We must perform a ceremony—"

"I'm not marrying him or something, am I?" I blurt out, suddenly worried about what I might have walked —*swam*—into by mistake.

"Of course not. A mer prince cannot marry a human girl," the queen remarks haughtily. "All you have to do is stay there and Quay will do the rest. We're here as witnesses."

She spreads her arms out in front of her, motioning to the sea floor we're hovering over. Quay slowly backs out of my line of sight, but the queen demands my attention.

"Go prepare yourself for your test, son. Cara," she addresses me, "you look lovely. I see my son has taken you to our guest closet. Do you like your headpiece?"

"Yes, your majesty."

"It's very fitting for the ceremony," she says. "All of my sons have been through this on their eighteenth birthdays, though I think today will be different with your presence."

"I can come back if you'd like to keep it—"

"No child, we wouldn't have it any other way," the queen quickly cuts me off. "My son must perform a special ceremony, you see. All mer princes must complete the ceremony on their eighteenth year of birth."

She motions me forward.

"Come, join me."

I swim forward, unsure of what to do. She reaches out her hand to me, long fingers beckoning me closer. Placing my hand in her's, she pulls me toward her throne.

"Now, jellyfish, Quay will need help with this. It's tradition to ask someone from the room to join him—he will choose you—you're the most lovely one here." I blush at her remarks. "He and I will guide you. Just follow along—this will go a long way toward getting you back to your parents too."

I turn as Quay enters the room again, this time, singing. His shoulder armor is now covered in blue shells, similar to mine. Pearls stretch across his chest from one shoulder to another.

"It's time to begin the Sinking," the queen announces as happily as if she'd just been handed a winning lottery ticket.

It's a strange name for a ceremony, but whatever.

Quay dances in the water, spinning in a way so that his hair flies out from him. It dips gracefully in the water. The sword on his belt loops out majestically as he moves. Some of the mermaids in the audience sway along with him, humming with his words. The shells move with him, dancing over his body.

"Each of my sons has taken a turn trying to complete the ceremony, starfish," the queen whispers in my ear.

"They've all failed. Tonight, Quay will try to complete the ceremony—he's come farther than any of my other sons have come, and I have great hopes for him."

She pushes my back, sending me into the open waters of the throne room toward Quay. He notices and swims over to me, never breaking his song.

Quay holds a hand to me and I tentatively take it. He guides me to the center of the room, singing an enchanting song. His voice is so lovely that I begin to wonder if he's a siren in disguise.

I sway with him as he guides me through the water. It's almost like prom night again as the last rays of light dance through the hole in the roof, sparkling against bits of debris in the water.

Definitely like prom.

Quay slows us, pulling me closer to him. He places my hands on his collarbone and draws me to him. His singing stops but the other mer pick up the tune, enchanting the waters with their voices.

"Cara," he murmurs, looking deep into my eyes.

The queen said it wasn't a marriage ceremony, but this is getting awfully romantic. I swallow hard, wondering how to put some space between us.

"Three of my sons have tried to complete the Sinking," the queen announced, breaking the trance. She swims toward us. "Three have failed and paid with their lives. Tonight, Quay will not fail.

"My son has brought a human to this palace as the curse foretold he must," she continues.

My skin prickles under the water—I was *brought* here.

Quay's grip around me tightens as his face goes slack.

No. Bad.

"My sons have been cursed since their childhood," the queen continues. "They've been doomed to die on the eve of their eighteenth year—"

"I'm sorry, Cara," Quay whispers.

I struggle to free myself.

"—if they did not complete the Sinking," the queen swims toward us as I pull back. Quay clamps down on my wrists and I worry they might shatter.

"Settle, anemone," the sea queen lectures me.

Anemone.

My mind flashes back to a few hours ago when the old woman pawned that necklace off on me—only it wasn't an old woman—it was the sea queen in disguise. She *planned this.*

"Why am I here?" I yell, struggling to get away from Quay. I pull one hand free, desperately trying to claw him off of my other wrist. Tears spring to my eyes but all they do is leak out into the water surrounding me.

"Quay, let me go!" I beg, sobbing.

"The last son of the reigning queen must break the curse by midnight or he too shall perish."

"Break the curse," the audience cheers, lending their support to the prince.

He pulls on me.

"Quay, please," I duck my head as I beg, hoping he'll see my fear and spare me.

If it's his life or mine, there's no way I'll win.

"Quay, please, you promised you'd help me. You saved me before."

"He saved you, child, because I instructed him to," the queen silences me, grabbing my chin and forcing me to look at her. "The curse says the princes must Sink a human in the heart of the sea before midnight on the day of his birth.

"Until this point, no human has survived the trip to the heart of the sea—the palace—and I've lost three other sons to this curse. I will not lose Quay, not even for *your* sake. I'm sorry you have to give your life for this, but I'll see to it that your family finds your body when we're done, legs back in place."

"You horrible witch!" I scream, still pulling against Quay, hoping to save my life. Though, even *if* I free myself, one of the other mer will stop me.

These mermaids and mermen will see to it that I drown in the heart of their kingdom to save their prince's life.

"I've done bad things in my life," the queen admits, "but always to help my collection or my sons. I'm sorry I had to trick you and bring you into the sea, but it's the only way to save my son's life, and I regret nothing if it means he lives past tonight."

I understand the need to protect loved ones, but she's murdering me to do it. She threw me into the sea and transformed me into a mermaid just to bring me to my death.

"Cara, stop struggling," Quay commands gently.

"I have a family," I shriek. "I have parents and a brother and a little cousin who depend on me. I'm going to college next year and I'm saving for a car to get there. I get straight A grades in all of my classes and I volunteer at the animal shelter twice a month. Please!"

"I can tell you are a good person, child, but it makes no difference," the queen responds lifelessly. "Quay must kill a human in the heart of the sea and he must do it now to survive. Thank you for your sacrifice."

"No!" I pull, ripping my hand away from Quay.

"Take her necklace," the queen instructs as I struggle.

"I cannot," Quay says, hands up as if he were surrendering. "I cannot kill the girl, Mother, I'm sorry."

"You *can* and you *will,* Quay. You will not leave us tonight. I've gone through far too much and given up everything for you to survive—you can't let her go!"

"I can't kill her, Mother," Quay looks devastated as I look over my shoulder, swimming to the door. A merman stops me. I try to dart around him, but can't.

"I have paid with my life for this, Quay. Both of our lives will be in vain if you don't do this now," she screeches. The other mer look horrified at her revelation.

"I care about her," he says quietly. I want to gag.

"You can't be in love with her, you idiot, you've known her for three hours."

"I didn't say *love*, Mother, but I'm drawn to her."

"She's a human," his mother protests. "And you both will be dead by morning—she'll never make it out of the sea. You must do this and live. I'll find you another to be drawn to."

Quay swims quietly toward me. I bite back a sob, grinding my teeth so hard that I can't hear anymore as my body shakes with the effort. I writhe violently as the merman holds my wrists.

"Hold still," I read Quay's lips. He comes at me with a knife in hand. Even if I can reach his sword, I doubt I'll make it in time.

Quay takes my hands from the merman blocking the door and roughly pulls me away. He turns back to his mother, knife still raised at me.

This is it. My life is over.

I spent my childhood dreaming of being a mermaid and now I will die as one. My family will find my body washed up along the beach somewhere and I will be gone forever.

Quay turns back to me, obviously having said something to his mer friends.

"Go," he commands, pushing me at the door.

I stare.

"Go!" he shouts, turning back to fight off any mer that challenge him. His shoulders hunch in pain, but I don't care one bit about what ails him.

I don't question his willingness to die at the hands of whatever curse he suffers from. I swim. I dart around the palace, desperate to find the door. When I do, I push my way to freedom in the almost-dark of night.

I have no idea where I'm going or where to swim.

The queen said I wouldn't survive the night and she also said she'd paid for this with her life, so I assume that means whatever she did to curse me into this form probably won't last longer than a few hours.

I need to make sure I can get to the surface, but I'm also aware that the higher I am, the easier I am to spot in the distance.

I swim. I don't know where, I don't know how far, but I swim as hard as I can.

When I feel faint, I bury myself in a kelp forest and pray none of the mer think to look there. I hear them in the distance as they search for the human girl who will trade her life for the life of their prince.

He can drown for all I care.

Things glow in the dark—fish and jellyfish that capture their prey by drawing them in with their light.

That's what Quay did to me—drew me in with his light.

Too bad the merman had fangs after all—rows and rows of vicious teeth under the chiseled façade.

Stop thinking about him, I command myself.

"Stay quiet," Quay's voice fills my head—a trick my mind is playing on me.

"Go away," I mutter at the vision. "Traitor."

"I tried to save you, I'm not a traitor," Quay says, appearing next to me. I scream as he clamps his hand over my mouth.

"Quiet, Cara," he demands. "I'm here to help you. I'll take you back."

"You mean you'll kill me," I wrench away from him. "This is just another part of your plan, isn't it, you eel?"

"I look like an eel to you?" he frowns.

"You look like a murderer," I reply, trying to find an escape.

"Cara, I wouldn't have let you go if I didn't intend on saving you. It isn't fair that you should die for me. I'll go to be with my brothers—it's a fate I've already reconciled with for myself. I had hope of survival for a few hours but I could never hurt you like that."

He looks sincere, but I don't believe a word he says.

"Let me take you back to your home," he requests. "We have to hurry before your tail wears off and you can no longer breathe underwater."

I *knew* it.

"I'll protect you from my mother and the others. They'll be all right without me—they already said good-bye. I'll take you to shore and then I'll return and make my peace with my fate on my own."

He's good. He's really good.

"Why don't you make your peace *over there*," I point. "I don't want your help."

"You need my help to return to land, Cara. You don't know where to go."

Moonlight sparkles down through the water, casting an eerie look over the merman. I nearly want to reach out and brush his long hair back from his face, but then I remember that he is the enemy.

"I will not willingly give my life up to you," I tell him.

"I'm not asking you to, Cara," he replies. "I just want you to let me fix what my mother has done to protect me. It is my duty to make it right. Let me do this one thing before the curse takes me."

I have no choice. I don't know how to get home, the glowing creatures are out to get me, and I'll die with or without Quay by my side, so I might as well drown while staring at his abs.

"Fine," I grumble.

He darts away from me, whispering for me to follow. I take off after him, racing through the dark.

I stay close to his tail so that I don't lose him in the darkness. I glide into his slipstream, making it easier to keep up.

"What was supposed to happen to me, Quay?" I ask bitterly.

"I was supposed to take your necklace," he says quietly. He looks like he wants to stop to talk to me, but we can't risk pausing and being found. "When removed, it takes away your ability to breath underwater—you turn back into a human.

"At that point, I was supposed to drown you," he concludes.

"I suppose you were going to add your own dramatic flair?" I question.

"My back up plan was to kiss you and try to give you enough air to get you to the surface," he admits, "if that is what you mean by flair."

I most certainly do *not* want to kiss him—but his lips are so enchanting.

"Hurry, Cara, we need to get you to the shore."

"How often do you go to the shore?" I ask, trying to learn anything I can use against him later.

"Never. It is forbidden."

"But you found me today," I protest.

"My mother sent me to fetch you. The only time we go to the shore is to get the human we need for the ceremony. Her plan succeeded this time—or would have if I could have followed it," he says dismally. "I just knew I couldn't live with myself with your blood on my hands."

"You said you felt drawn to me," I comment. "What does that mean?"

"I don't know," he replies. "I feel we have a connection. That's all I can tell you."

A noise sounds in the distance—the mermen are coming for us.

"We need to hide," Quay says, looking around. "There. A cavern."

He grabs my hand, pulling me down in the water whether I like it or not. I allow him to swim us into the cave.

Inside, we find a darkness so overwhelming that it's a shock to the system when light begins to glow around us.

"Bioluminescence," he informs me. "When the algae is disturbed, that happens."

Everything glows around us as we hover in the water.

"They can't see it outside, can they?" I ask.

"No, we're too far inside the cave."

He enfolds me in his arms, holding me to his chest. I

try not to cringe, though I keep my elbows firmly in place between him and me in case I need to push him away.

His hand settles on the small of my back around the spikes and frilly pieces of my tail—I honestly don't know how mermaids deal with this. It's one thing to have fins at the bottom, but extra offshoots everywhere?

It's pretty, but not worth it.

His fingers graze one of the fins making me gasp. I can't tell if it's horrifying or if it's incredible.

"I truly am sorry, Cara," he murmurs.

"So you've said."

He sighs.

"I'm willing to die to protect you, Cara. I hope you'll remember that one day when you think of me."

I'll be sure to thank him in my speech before the police check me into a facility for a seventy-two-hour hold after I tell them about all this.

"Stay here, I'll go check."

I grab his wrist, eyes wide.

"I'm not bringing them back here, Cara," he groans. "If I were going to kill you in front of them, I would have done it at the palace. If I needed to kill you in the cavern, I would have brought you directly here instead of to my mother. I am on your side."

He swims away, leaving me in the glow of the cave.

He makes a good point.

Still, I look for anything I can use as a weapon should I need it.

When he returns, he's alone.

"They're gone," he announces, holding out his hand. "We need to move faster or we won't make it in time."

Time for me to turn back into a human or time for him to die? Maybe both.

"When will I….*transform*?" I ask as we swim back into the ocean.

"Soon," he replies. "We don't have long."

"Will my transformation and your…um, death be at the same time?"

"I do not know, but I don't think so. I believe you'll transform first. I have until the end of the day, but I don't think your necklace will hold you much longer, which is why we need to swim faster. Please, Cara. I'm sure you're exhausted and you're still learning your tail, but please hurry."

He sounds terrified that we're not going fast enough. I push, flipping my tail as hard as I can. My control over direction leaves something to be desired, but with my hand in his, I manage to go in the right direction, despite bumping into him several times.

"Quay," I gasp, finding it hard to breathe. "I have to slow down."

I cough, trying to catch my breath.

"No," he whispers in shock, halting. He adds dismally,"It's time."

"What?" I squeak out between coughs.

"You're turning back into a human, Cara. Hold on, I have to get you to the surface."

He grabs me around the waist, practically throwing me over his shoulder as he darts toward the waves overhead. I start gagging, choking on the water as I transform.

Everything hurts as my scales tear away from me.

I scream in pain.

"Hold on, Cara," he instructs as water goes up my nose, burning the entire inside of my head. "Almost there."

My nails dig into his back as I fight to survive.

Just as I think I'm going to black out, we hit the air.

My hair flops in front of my face and I fight to free myself from my new prison. Quay holds tightly to me with one arm and pokes at my face with his other hand, trying to help part my hair enough that air can enter my lips and heal my lungs.

I cough, spitting up water.

"You're safe," he murmurs, rubbing my back with the hand he was using to help with my hair. "You're on the surface now. You're safe."

I cling to him, letting him soothe me.

Miraculously, the merman saved me.

"Shh," he says softly. "We still have to get you home. Calm yourself down and try to breathe normally."

When I finally take my face out of his neck where I buried it, all I see is water. I look back at him in horror.

"We didn't quite make it, but I'll get you there," he promises.

He scoops my legs up in his arms and carries me toward the horizon, swimming on the surface.

"It's over there," he says. "It's just hard to see in the dark."

I see a space where the reflection on the water ends, and I assume that's land, but in the immense darkness, I can't be sure.

After a while, he struggles to stay above the water.

"Are you okay?"

"We don't swim up here much," he grunts in reply. "It's hard to stay above water."

"I can swim on my own—you can go back under."

"I'm not leaving you. We've come this far, and since this is the last thing I do, I want to do it right."

I notice part of my dress is still wrapped around me, covering my legs—I'm incredibly grateful whatever curse had wrapped me in scales had used my own garments to assist in the transformation.

"Then swim under the water next to me," I reply, wondering how many times I'm going to panic, thinking he's a shark about to bite me.

"No, we're fine," he pants. "We'll make it."

He dips lower in the water. I drop my hand into the ocean behind him and cup water onto his shoulders.

"Does this help?"

He smiles sadly at me.

"You're kind, Cara," he responds.

So, no, it's not helping. He doesn't stop me though, so I keep going, knowing it's meaningful to him that I'm trying to be helpful.

I pause between handfuls of water, not wanting to over do it. Every time the water touches his skin his lips tick up, or his eyes soften for a moment, closing slightly as he gives himself over to the water.

"I made the right choice," he says at one point during our journey. "You are the one that should live, Cara."

"So should live too, Quay."

There's no way I'm giving up my life for this though, so let's not even go there.

"You don't deserve this," I add. "You're a good merman."

"None of us deserved this, but it's our fate—our curse."

"There must be *something* that we can do," I protest. "There *has* to be a way to stop this."

"There is nothing that can stop this," he says sadly. "I wish though, that I had a chance to get to know you better, Cara of land."

"Funny, I was thinking the same thing about you,

Quay, prince of the sea."

His smile nearly breaks my heart.

Quay looks behind me, smile morphing into relief.

"We're here," he says. "Just in time."

I turn to look, and he twitches under my movements.

The shore is there, right in front of me. I might even be able to reach the bottom if I put my feet down, though, with the waves, I don't dare let go of the merman carrying me to safety.

I slide my fingers across his shoulders, not wanting to say goodbye yet.

"Quay," I say, turning back to him.

He hunches over in the water, dipping me low into the waves. I gasp for air, reliving my transformation.

"Quay!" I shout as he starts to convulse.

"Go, Cara," he replies, pushing me away from him.

A wave catches me, hurdling me toward the shore as Quay shudders in the water.

"What's happening?" I demand, trying to get back to him.

"Go home, Cara," he tries to wave me off.

"Quay!"

"It's happening," he replies, heartbroken. "I don't want you to see me like this, please go."

"I'm not leaving you," I fight my way through the waves. "You took me home—now I'll take you home."

He starts thrashing in the water, bobbing up and

down in the waves. He's tossed like a buoy indicating the end of the swimming area in the ocean.

When I finally reach him, his entire body shakes.

I wonder if my transformation had looked this terrifying.

Wrapping an arm around him, I try to stabilize him in the water to make it the least painful I can. I can barely touch the bottom so I attempt to drag him into where I won't potentially drown.

"Quay, I'm here."

He reaches around me, attempting to ground himself with my body, using me as an anchor. His body twitches as his tail whips in the water around me.

Quay grunts, groaning in pain with every movement. He looks like he's snapping to the beat of a charged AED machine and someone is trying to revive him with panels on his chest. I nearly expect someone to scream *clear!*

His feet kick up from the water for a moment plunging back down into the black depths of the rough line of shells in the water. I hold tighter to him, just wanting to make his passing easier.

Wait.

Feet?

Sweet sunrise, the boy has legs!

"Quay!" I shout over the roar of the waves. "You have legs!"

His eyes pinch shut in pain.

"I know," he replies through gritted teeth.

"You're turning into a human?" I gape.

He attempts to nod, letting out a strangled yell of pain.

"Quay, you're human!" I repeat. "You're not dead, you're a human."

"They all turned…" he groans, "into humans and drowned."

"But you're not below the sea," I remind him, barely loosening my grip on his waist. "You're on land, Quay. You can't drown here."

"We're all cursed to die," he moans, convulsions slowing. "It will happen anyway, even above the sea."

"You're not going to die, Quay," I reply. "I've got you."

His breathing steadies as he practices long, deep breaths for the first time in his life. When he calms down, I brush his hair back as he leans back in my arms.

"I think you're safe, Quay. I think you survived."

"Go home, Cara. I'll be fine," he insists, still thinking he's going to keel over dead in front of me.

I duck down in the water with him.

"We're safe, your highness," I giggle. "We can reach out to your mother and let her know you're well. I mean, I don't particularly like her at this point since she's still trying to murder me, but maybe the fact that you didn't die in her palace will change her mind about me."

He finally focuses his piercing blue eyes on me.

His hands are wrapped around my shoulder and I reach up to move a lock of his shell-beaded hair back.

"You're safe. I'm safe. You saved me and now we're both free."

"*You* saved *me,* Cara. I honestly don't know how, but you did. " He puts his hand on his chest. "Thank you."

"We should get out of the water," I reply. Dark means feeding time for the small sharks that like to eat toward shore, and the last thing I need is to have something bite off Quay's new legs.

I move us toward the shore, helping him to get his feet under himself as we near a level where we'd either have to start walking or resort to crawling in on our knees.

The water slaps my backside before I can straighten and nearly sends me head first into the sand. I catch myself on Quay who hasn't found his land legs yet and nearly topples with me.

Thankfully his transformation has left him with something that looks a bit like a faded blue kilt wrapped around his waist. I help him up onto the shore where we both collapse.

Breathing is hard as we sit together, me curled up on his chest, tucked under his arm, and Quay sprawled out on his back. When we calm down, we're left under the stars with the ocean waves beating against the sand a few feet away.

"So," he breaks the silence. "This is land."

"This is land," I repeat, reaching up to rip the necklace off of my neck. "Looks like I'm about to have a lot to show you, Prince Quay."

He nods, taking it all in as his hand finds it's way to my hip, wrapped around my back as he cradles me against him.

I'm sure the world up here will be shocking to him.

The sand crunches in my hair—I'm going to need a hot shower when I get home to fix my salt-and-sand-crusted body. It's amazing how I can climb out of one body of water and desperately want to slip into another.

"I have a feeling I'm going to have a lot of explaining to do too," I reply. "Time to get our stories straight—I'm thinking that I dropped the necklace and got sucked out to sea and you were passing by on a canoe and fished me out of the drink."

Is it possible for him to *smell* like the sea?

"The drink?"

"The ocean," I correct myself. I'm really going to have to stop using half my vocabulary around the merman—around the *man*. "You can stay with my family until we figure out what to do about all of this. Maybe your mother can sell her soul again and get new magic to turn you back into a merman."

"Perhaps," he sounds skeptical. "I would like to see your world though, Cara."

"I'd like to show you." I pause for a moment, thinking through the day. "Hey, my wish on the starfish came true."

"Mine too," he chuckles for the first time since we climbed onto the sand. "Even my second and third wish came true."

"Oh? What was that?"

"My first wish was to survive the day. I have done that," he says. "My second wish was for my mother to not be able to silence you with the Sinking and here you are. And you already know my third wish."

"Do I?" I challenge.

"You had the same wish. To know each other better."

My eyes grow wide.

With my hand on his chest, rising in the air each time he takes a breath, and head curled into his strong shoulder that is surprisingly lacking in shoulder armor, I realize he's right—I'm glad I get to learn more about this mysterious merman.

A voice calls for me in the distance, searching for me well into the night.

"Uh oh," I add. "Time to go. Don't forget the story—you rescued me and we just made it back to shore."

He nods, allowing me to help pull him up—he's still not used to carrying his body weight and not being able to float everywhere.

"Ready to meet my family, your highness?"

About K.M. Robinson

K.M. Robinson is a storyteller who creates new worlds both in her writing and in her fine arts conceptual photography. She is a marketing, branding and social media strategy educator who is recognized at first sight by her very long hair. She is a creative who focuses on photography, videography, couture dress making, and writing to express the stories she needs to tell. She almost always has a camera within reach. Visit her at her website for free books and exclusive samples: www.kmrobinsonbooks.com

CONNECT ON SOCIAL MEDIA

facebook.com/kmrobinsonbooks

instagram.com/kmrobinsonbooks

twitter.com/kmrobinsonbooks

youtube.kmrobinsonbooks.com

Get free books and excerpts of other K.M. Robinson books at excerpt.kmrobinsonbooks.com

ALSO BY K.M. ROBINSON

The Jaded Duology

Book One: Jaded

Book Two: Risen

The Golden Trilogy

Book One: Golden

Forged: A Golden Novella

Book Two: Locked

Book Three: Edge

The Legends Chronicles

Along Came A Spider: A Prequel Novelette

And They'll Come Home: A Prequel Novelette

Virtually Sleeping Beauty: A Novella Retelling

The Siren Wars Saga

Book One: The Siren Wars

Book Two: Darker Depths (Coming June 2018)

Book Three: Beyond The Shores (Coming July 2018)

The Revolution Of Jack Frost (Coming Nov 2018)

SPECIAL THANKS

Special thanks to all of our readers, we couldn't have done this without you!
We hope you enjoyed the Of The Deep Anthology as much as we enjoyed creating it for you!

To see the incredible artwork by our highly skilled artists that goes with the book in color, please visit www.crescentseapublishing.com/ofthedeep

Anthologies

To get involved in our upcoming
Crescent Sea Publishing Anthologies,
please visit www.crescentseapublishing.com/anthologies

To see the artwork from this book in color, please visit
mermaids.crescentseapublishing.com
to access our Anthology World Portal
with exclusive behind the scenes from the anthology.

www.ingramcontent.com/pod-product-compliance
Lightning Source LLC
Chambersburg PA
CBHW030518310726
48979CB00010B/1723/J